ENDORSEMENTS

"A DELICIOUS AND DELIGHTFUL STORY WITH A LARGE HELPING OF FUN AND A DASH OF ROMANCE."
~ JENNIFER BECKSTRAND, AWARD-WINNING AUTHOR OF THE MATCHMAKERS OF HUCKLEBERRY HILL SERIES

"I LIKED THE HAPPY ENDING AND WOULD LIKE TO SEE MORE OF THESE CHARACTERS IN OTHER BOOKS BY THIS AUTHOR."
~ AMAZON REVIEWS

" I WOULD RECOMMEND THIS BOOK TO ANYONE WANTING A QUICK READ, GOOD CLEAN READING."
~ AMAZON REVIEWS

"JUST THE RIGHT LENGTH AND I ENJOYED IT AS A INSPIRATIONAL STORY."
~ AMAZON REVIEWS

"I WAS PULLED INTO THE STORY FROM THE VERY FIRST SENTENCE, AND COULDN'T PUT IT DOWN UNTIL I FINISHED THE LAST SENTENCE. FORTUNATELY, IT IS A RATHER SHORT BOOK AND DIDN'T TAKE LONG TO FINISH."
~ AMAZON REVIEWS

" A DELIGHTFUL STORY YOU'LL NOT WANT TO PUT DOWN UNTIL YOU FINISH IT. YOU WILL TURN EACH PAGE AND WONDER WHAT WILL HAPPEN NEXT. NAOMI MILLER IS A TALENTED AND WONDERFUL AUTHOR, AND I CAN'T WAIT TO READ MORE OF HER STORIES."
~ MOLLY JEBBER, AUTHOR OF *LIZA'S SECOND C̶H̶A̶N̶C̶E̶*

ABOUT THE SWEET SHOP MYSTERY SERIES

BOOKS BY NAOMI MILLER

Amish Sweet Shop Mystery

Blueberry Cupcake Mystery

Christmas Cookie Mystery

Lemon Tart Mystery

Pumpkin Pie Mystery

Chocolate Truffle Mystery

Peach Cobbler Mystery

❋ The Abbott Creek Cookbook

Amish Sweet Shop Romance

Coffee Bean Connection

Warm Peppermint Kisses
(Releasing Winter 2024)

Windy Gap Wishes

A Mother For Leah

A Suitor For Rebekah

PLAIN FAIRY TALES

ASHES TO AMISH

HER BEASTLY BLESSING

CHILLED TO THE CORE
(RELEASING WINTER 2024)

CHILDREN'S BOOKS

SOPHIE FINDS A FAMILY

SOPHIE CELEBRATES THANKSGIVING

SOPHIE'S NEW HOME

SOPHIE TAKES A WALK

coffee
BEAN
connection
AMISH SWEET SHOP ROMANCE

To God
be the Glory...

coffee BEAN connection

AMISH SWEET SHOP ROMANCE

INTERNATIONAL BESTSELLING AUTHOR

NAOMI MILLER

A NOTE FROM NAOMI MILLER

Coffee Bean Connection was a story I've wanted to write for a while... sweet, helpful Hannah has been very patient, waiting for her story to be written... and here it is!

Although I aim for stories that are fun to read, and full of joy, compassion, forgiveness, and friendship... I couldn't wait to write Hannah's story... and what happens when her life gets turned upside down after The Coffee Cup is sold to a stranger.

As with any work of fiction, I've taken license in some areas of research as a means of creating circumstances necessary to my characters or plot. I've created fictional characters in a fictional town. Any inaccuracies portrayed in this book are completely due to fictional license.

God bless you!

~Naomi

GLOSSARY

The German/Dutch dialect spoken by the Amish is not a written language. It is solely dependent on the location and origin of each settlement. The spellings below are approximations.

allrecht = all right
appeditlich = delicious
bopli/boplin = baby/babies
bruder/bruders = brother/brothers
buwe/buwes = boy/boys
danki = thank you
Dat = dad
dochder = daughter
du bischt daheem = you're home
Englischer = non-Amish person
frau = wife
froh = happy
Gott = God
Gudemariye = Good morning
gut = good
hochmut = pride
hungrich = hungry
in lieb = in love
jah = yes
kaffe = coffee
kapp = cap

kichlin = kitchen
kinner = children
kumme = come
maedel/maedels = girl/girls
Mamm = mom
naerfich = nervous
nee = no
rumschpringe = running around time for youth
schweschder/schweschders = sister/sisters
verrickt = crazy
Was iss letz = What's wrong
wunderbaar = wonderful

To every thing there is a season,
and a time to every purpose under the
heaven.

A time to be born, and a time to die,
a time to plant, and a time to pluck up
that which is planted.

A time to love...

Ecclesiastes 3:1-2, 8a

For Rachel and Gwen, who continued to
encourage me even when I didn't want to do what
I was always meant to do.

And for my fans, who never gave up on me when
I stopped writing for a time.

This book is for you...

one

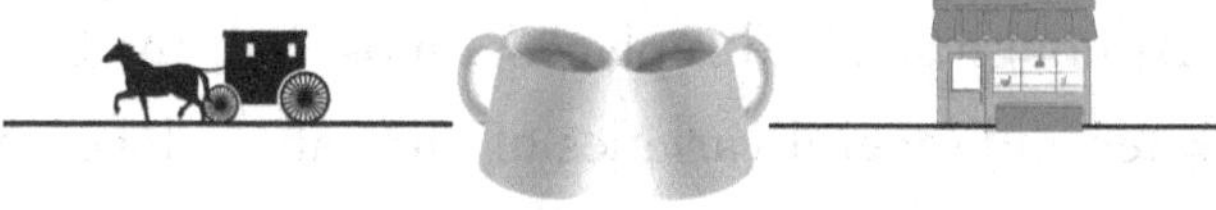

Monday morning at The Coffee Cup began as usual. Hannah Kaufman arrived promptly at five thirty A.M. to give herself thirty minutes to prep the shop and brew the delicious coffees they sold to their customers.

As the aroma of fresh *kaffe* filled the room, Hannah took a moment to sniff the air in the shop. For some reason, the *kaffe* always seemed to smell even more delicious in the cool autumn mornings. Their customers must feel the same way, because more *kaffe* was purchased in the fall than during the hot summer days.

Looking at the clock over the front door, Hannah stepped away from the *kaffe* and hurried to stock the shelves in the glass cases with cookies, pastries, and flaky croissants, before moving to the refrigerated area. Stopping in front of the glass doors, she quickly checked for empty spaces.

Although she had replaced almost half the bottles of water and several varieties of juice after closing last night, she made it a point to always check again before opening the shop. Thankfully everything was as it should be and the shelves were full.

Next she tended to the counter space where the full carafes of brewed *kaffe* would be placed. She filled the napkin dispensers, then checked to see that there were plenty of choices available for customers who used sweeteners, half and half, or flavored creamers in the hot drinks they ordered.

For years, Mr. Dell had ordered cookies and pastries from a large bakery in the city, but recently, the delivery truck had failed to arrive on time—again. Hannah had been forced to rush across the street to The Sweet Shop and purchase whatever she could from her friend Katie Chupp, who had worked at the bakery for several years. While she was there, Hannah had placed an order for what the coffee shop would need for the rest of the day and a separate order for items needed for the following day.

After his customers had purchased more than they normally did and the coffee shop had run out of baked goods in record time, Mr. Dell had decided to continue to purchase his cookies, croissants and pastries from Mrs. O'Neal's bakery.

After all, The Sweet Shop was the best choice all around, since it was located just across the street from the coffee shop. Mrs. O'Neal was a good business woman and someone you could count on. Every afternoon, Travis Davis would deliver whatever they ordered for the following day before he headed out to make his other deliveries.

When Hannah first began working at The Coffee Cup, it had seemed strange to her that their shop would sell some of the same things The Sweet Shop did. After all, the coffee shop was located right across the street from the bakery.

But she soon learned that many of their customers who came in for hot drinks didn't want to have to visit two different stores, especially early in the morning on their way to work. Therefore, it made sense to sell a few choice baked items along with the drinks they sold to customers.

Whenever Hannah called to place their order, she and Bella would usually end up laughing at the idea that Katie's *wunderbaar* baking was sold in not one... not two... but three different locations now.

The Sweet Shop was the main location, of course. Mr. O'Neal at the Irish Blessings Cafe had begun selling Katie's desserts, as well as using her delicious breads, almost from the first day he had opened his cafe. And now The Coffee Cup was selling her desserts, too.

Of course, most everyone seemed to know that the *wunderbaar* breads and tasty treats came from The Sweet Shop. Hannah couldn't remember how many times she had heard customers mention Katie.

"I'll have a couple of croissants and a dozen oatmeal raisin cookies. Tell Katie I sure appreciate how hard she works. That girl for sure has a gift for baking."

"Give me a couple of cookies to go with my coffee. I declare, I don't know why Charlie Dell ever wasted his time with that place in the city. Nothing beats Katie's baking."

And, of course, Mayor Robertson almost always

stopped by on his way to work for coffee and treats.

"Hmm. Give me half a dozen of Katie's croissants today... and a container of cream cheese. Everyone at works looks forward to break time whenever I bring snacks that Katie Chupp makes."

Mr. Dell had been delighted to find that he continued to sell even more croissants and pastries than when he had ordered them from the supplier in the city. Mrs. O'Neal gave him a better discount, too.

Looking up at the clock on the wall and seeing that it was almost six o'clock, Hannah hurried over to turn on the lights, unlock the door, and turn the sign around so that it would read "OPEN", then quickly moved behind the counter to wait for the first customer, who had opened the door and was heading her way.

Monday was about to get very busy.

Two hours later, Mr. Dell, looking a bit flustered, walked into the coffee shop. Hannah wondered what could be wrong. Mr. Dell had looked a bit stressed during the past few months, but as he didn't discuss his business or personal life with Hannah, she had no idea what might be causing it—or if there was anything she could do to help.

"Good morning, Hannah. Did you have a nice weekend?"

"*Jah*, it was *gut*. Did you enjoy your weekend?" Hannah hoped his reply would be a *gut* one, but lately Mr. Dell had been more than a little moody and she wasn't quite sure what to expect from him.

"Yes. Well, actually no. No I didn't. Not really." Mr. Dell hesitated a few seconds before he continued. "I've been worried about my brother for quite some time. He's been getting steadily worse and he wants me to come stay with him."

"Oh, I'm so sorry to hear that your *bruder* is sick." Hannah said, with a tone of sympathy in her voice.

Mr. Dell poured himself a cup of coffee, then turned toward Hannah, motioning her to join him at a nearby table. After sitting down, he took a few sips of his coffee before speaking.

"He's not sick. Well, not exactly. He has some health problems, but nothing life threatening. Not at the moment, anyway. Although it could become worse. He has rheumatoid arthritis, he's diabetic, and he's old. He tends to lose his balance easily and I've been worried that I'd probably get a call from the hospital any day now." He smiled. "I'm not getting any younger, either. That's what I wanted to discuss with you. He wants me to come live with him."

"But doesn't he live in Florida? I mean, isn't that where you go every so often to visit your *bruder*?" Hannah looked perplexed. "Unless you have another *bruder* who lives there."

"Nope. That's the one. Ben lives in a small town near Miami. He moved there almost ten years ago after he retired. Said he'd always planned to retire to Florida, where it's warmer in the winter than any other state, except perhaps Texas or parts of Southern California."

"And you're truly thinking of leaving Illinois and moving to Florida? Leaving all your friends?" Hannah could hardly believe what she was hearing.

Mr. Dell smiled. "Well, that's the other part of my news. I figure now is as good a time as any to retire, so I told my brother I'd move in with him. We're both widowers, and we can take care of each other."

Clearing his throat, he took a sip of his coffee before going on. "I'll tell you, Hannah, I'm looking forward to enjoying warm, sunny weather this winter, instead of the snow and ice we get here every year."

"But Mr. Dell, what about your coffee shop? Are you planning to open a coffee shop there? And will you be closing The Coffee Cup?" What would you do about your business?"

Mr. Dell didn't answer for a moment. Hannah started to speak again, but had no idea what to say, so she sat quietly, hoping her boss would say something. Thankfully, she didn't have to wait long.

"I should have talked to you about this sooner, but I didn't want to say anything until I knew it would work out." Mr. Dell hesitated, looking a bit abashed. "I put my house up for sale. The agent said it shouldn't take long to find a buyer. And I'm selling the business. As of Friday, someone else will own The Coffee Cup. You'll have a new boss."

Hannah felt as if she was about to cry. She was glad there was no one else in the coffee shop right then. What should she say? What should she do? She felt her face redden, but still she sat quietly, not knowing what to do.

"Hannah, I know this must be a shock for you, but you have nothing to worry about. I've spoken to the new owner and he doesn't plan to make any changes right now. He doesn't plan to replace you or anything. On the contrary, he feels strongly that you should stay. He said it's important to him that nothing change right away, until he gets the lay of the land."

Immediately Hannah felt relieved, yet she knew Mr. Dell would hear the nervousness in her voice. "So I'll continue to work here, just as I do now?"

"Absolutely. I was prepared to help you find another job if things hadn't worked out the way they did, but I really don't think you need to worry about your job." Mr. Dell looked considerably better now. "I don't mind telling you, I'm more than a little relieved that things here will be the same after I'm gone."

Finishing the last of his coffee, he stood up, pushed his chair back under the table, and patted Hannah's hand just before walking away. He walked through the door into the back room without turning around, as if it would be too difficult to look back.

Watching him as he headed into the back, most likely going to his office, Hannah just sat there, not wanting to think about how things might be changing soon. She was happy for Mr. Dell, and his *bruder*—who obviously wanted and needed him—but she was stunned by the sudden news that the shop had been sold.

Dear Gott, please bless Mr. Dell—and his bruder. And if it be your wille, please help me be able to keep my job here, and take away my fears and doubts... and help me to be a blessing to the new owner.

Feeling better after her prayer, Hannah returned to work, determined to give her best effort today. After all, who knew what would happen on Friday...

two

Katie Chupp was just finishing an order when Anna pushed through the swinging doors and entered the kitchen.

"Katie, you have a visitor. I told her you were busy, but she said not to rush, so I let her know that you would come out whenever you finish what you're working on and can take your break."

With a look of superiority, Anna turned and headed back to the main part of the bakery.

Katie smiled. A moment later, a giggle escaped

her lips. Trying hard to keep her laughter under control, Katie breathed a quick prayer.

Danki Gott, for Anna. Help me to remember what a help she is to me, and not to be getting upset with her.

Instead of letting Anna get to her, Katie tried to always remind herself how thankful she was that Anna was such a hard worker. After Bella cut her hours in half so she could spend more time at home with little Emma, Katie needed someone she could count on.

Anna was the *dochder* of Samuel and Liz Miller. Katie's *bruder* Noah had been apprenticed to Samuel for a couple of years, and now he worked with him full-time at his buggy shop.

Anna had no idea that anyone knew about her crush on Noah, Katie's *bruder*. Katie wasn't sure when Anna had begun to see Noah as more than just a friend, but after she started dating Travis Davis, it seemed obvious to her that Anna was smitten with Noah. Of course Katie hadn't said anything to Anna —or anyone else, for that matter—but she began watching her *bruder* for signs that he was interested in Anna, but so far he hadn't acted any different toward her but as a friend and neighbor.

Not that she saw Noah a lot. He was working full

time with Samuel Miller now, building and repairing the buggies that the church members used for transportation. It was for certain a big job and Noah came home tired much of the time. Sometimes he didn't even make it to the singings that most of the single, young people attended.

Katie wasn't for sure how she would feel to have Anna as a *schweschder*-in-law. Anna worked in the front of the bakery, taking care of the customers, while Katie worked in the kitchen, baking all sorts of delightful concoctions.

Anna, although a year younger than Katie, had recently begun to act as if she was older and wiser than Katie, and too often it felt as if she was looking down on her. Sometimes it even felt like Anna was judging her, especially now, since Katie had begun dating Travis, who was an *Englischer* and not a member of the Amish church.

Anna didn't bother mincing words when it came to telling Katie just what she thought of her decision to not join the church—and even worse, to get involved with an *Englischer*. Not long ago, after their church meeting and the lunch everyone enjoyed, Katie was helping clean the kitchen, when Anna stepped inside the kitchen and said as much to Katie.

She told her she was being sinful and that she should find a nice Amish boy to date, and obey her parents and be baptized and join the church.

After this, Katie noticed that Anna had begun to treat Travis and his younger *schweschder* Gwen as if they shouldn't be working at the bakery at all. Katie didn't know if Mrs. O'Neal had noticed or not, but she hadn't said anything about it, at least not to her.

After Mrs. O'Neal had hired Anna to work full-time recently at the bakery, Anna rarely said anything of a personal nature to Katie—at least while they were at work. And she was a *gut* worker.

Putting the order she had just finished in the walk-in cooler, Katie closed the door and pushed through the swinging doors into the bakery, surprised to find Hannah waiting for her.

"Katie, do you have lunch plans? If you don't, could we go to lunch together?"

"Sure, I can go now. Just let me go get my purse."

"You won't need it. It's my treat today."

"Well, *allrecht*, if you're sure."

"I'm sure. Come on, let's go."

Katie was amused when Hannah took her arm and pulled her across the street toward the Irish Blessings Cafe. It was a beautiful fall day and Katie stopped just outside the cafe to look toward the sky.

"Look at those clouds, Hannah. Have you ever seen such a *wunderbaar* sight?"

The day was a perfect example of autumn, with pumpkins decorating the town square, along with wheelbarrows filled with leaves of different colors — reds and yellows and oranges and browns and blacks. A few green leaves could be found, too, but not many.

"*Jah*, everything looks *wunderbaar*. The trees and the decorations and the smell of harvest in the air."

Still, Hannah looked a bit distracted, so Katie didn't argue when her friend pulled her toward the cafe. After sitting down at a table near the window, Katie turned to her friend.

"*Allrecht*, what's going on? I'm happy to have lunch together, and I love the sandwiches here, but you rarely ever take a lunch break away from The Coffee Cup. When you come into the bakery, it's usually to leave your order for the next day."

"*Ach*, Katie. I received some rather disturbing news today and I just had to get away from the shop for a little while and talk to someone. And you're my first choice, because you really care."

"Disturbing news? Whatever could it be?"

Just then, Ethan Lewis stopped at their table for their order. After placing orders for sandwiches, chips and sodas, they waited until he had walked away before continuing.

"I'm not sure if I'm supposed to talk about it, but Mr. Dell didn't say anything about it being a secret, so I guess it's *allrecht*."

Hannah stopped again as Ethan brought their sodas. As soon as he stepped away, she spoke again. "Katie, Mr. Dell is moving to Florida to live with his *bruder*. He's selling his house. And... and he has sold The Coffee Cup."

"What? And you had no idea until today?"

"*Nee,* not really. *Ach*, he's been a bit moody at times, and it seemed like he was under a bit of stress, but he has never said anything to me about moving or selling the cafe."

"So how did you find out?"

"Well, this morning when there were no more customers in the shop, he asked me to sit down and talk. Then he told me that his brother needed him to move in with him. He said that he was selling his house, that he had already sold The Coffee Cup and that Friday would be his last day there."

"So it's really decided? He is going for sure and for certain?"

"It for sure sounds that way to me."

"But what will happen to you? I could ask Mrs. O'Neal about your working at the bakery if you want."

"*Ach*, Mr. Dell said I don't need to be worrying about my job. He says that the new owner intends to keep The Coffee Cup pretty much the way it is now — and that my job is supposed to stay the same."

"That's *gut*. I hope it turns out the way he says, so it works out *allrecht* for everyone. But I am certain you will miss Mr. Dell. You have worked with him for many years." Katie swallowed the last bite of her sandwich. "Do you know anything about the new owner?"

"*Nee*, he didn't tell me anything about the sale or the new owner. I guess perhaps I will be meeting him, or her, on Friday."

"*Jah*, I guess so. Did he say —"

"Hiya Katie-girl. Hannah, it's good to see you. Did you ladies enjoy your lunch?" Mr. O'Neal smiled at them.

"It was *appeditlich*, as always." Hannah replied. "I need to get back to work, Katie. Can we talk later?"

"Of course. I should be going back to work, too. My boss will be angry with me if I'm late, doncha know."

Andrew laughed. "Now Katie, we both know Amelia dotes on you. I can't imagine her ever getting angry with you, especially over being a few minutes late."

Ethan walked over to the table with their bill. Before either girl could do anything, Andrew had reached out and grabbed it, then proceeded to rip it in half and handed it back to Ethan.

"Ethan, please dispose of this in the trash. These ladies work very hard and they deserve a treat now and then. It's been several weeks since I've had the chance to buy them lunch."

Turning back to the table, he winked at Katie and Hannah. "Ladies, your lunch is on me today. And I don't want to hear any discussion about it."

"But Mr. O'Neal, you —"

"Nay. Katie-girl, you and Hannah honor me with your friendship. Now let's talk of other things. How's sweet little Emma coming along? Each time I see her she's gotten bigger. She's not gonna be a wee babe much longer."

"*Nee*, she is growing so swiftly Bella has trouble keeping clothes to fit her. Mamm and some of the other ladies are staying busy making bigger outfits for her."

"I was more than a bit surprised to find that Bella was returning to work. If ye ask me, she belongs at home with the wee babe." Andrew looked as if he wasn't quite sure if he should be discussing this with Katie and Hannah.

After a moment, he went on. "I said as much to Milly, since she's Bella's employer, but she looked at me like I was not knowing what's what."

Katie wasn't sure how to respond. One the one hand, she didn't want to offend Mr. O'Neal. But she knew why Bella had returned to work... and she agreed with her reasons. Should she share them with Mr. O'Neal, or wait and let Bella tell him herself.

Finally, she decided to go ahead and tell him. "Mr. O'Neal, Bella shared her feelings with me about returning to work. Although it's difficult to leave young Emma, Bella feels that she's doing the right thing by working to support herself and her daughter. And she's only working part-time now. She's not planning to work full-time until Emma begins school."

"Aye, I was knowing that. But it doesn't quite set right with me. Oh, I'll do all right by her, because she's made her decision and it was her right to make it. But to leave such a tiny babe—"

Andrew looked as if he were going to jump up and leave, but instead he leaned in close to Katie, speaking softly to her.

"Did you know that I was married before, Katie? My dear wife and I married just out of school. Aye, and we longed for children, but it wasn't meant to be. Instead, after nineteen years of marriage the good Lord took Bridget and left me all alone. For seven long years, I got by, barely living, until I couldn't stand to be in the same place with all the memories of things that would never be."

Andrew stopped. He cleared his voice and took a deep breath before going on.

"I left Ireland then, determined to find a place to settle. And die. Instead, somehow I found Abbott Creek. And who was the first person I just happened to meet? My beloved Milly, that's who."

His eyes lit up as he spoke of his wife. "Of course, I had no idea of what the future held... that in just two short years I would be happily married to that remarkable woman. If I'd had any idea at the time, I'd have packed a bag and headed to Abbott Creek as fast as I could get here!"

Katie couldn't help but smile as she witnessed the look of love on his face as he closed his eyes and grew quiet. After a few moments, Andrew looked over at her and continued.

"Well, that's my story. Milly had just lost her Henry and she seemed just as lost as I felt. I stopped into the bakery to buy some bread and a few pastries —and there she was. We chatted a bit and I left. A few days later, I returned and we chatted again. I began to look forward to our chats, although I would never have admitted even to myself that I was smitten with her."

Katie was amazed that she had never heard anything about his first wife. His story was so sad, it made her feel like crying. She took several breaths and then gave him a shaky smile. "And when did you decide to open the cafe?"

"About six months after I moved here, the man who had tried to make a go of a home-style restaurant here decided to sell it and move away. Thinking it would be a grand thing to help me stay busy, plus meet people in the community, I snapped it up. I didn't much care if it would be a big success or not at the time, but once I got started making plans, I determined that it would be a good place for a sandwich shop and I could make a go of it if I really tried. It took about three months to get the renovations done. And it all worked out."

With a wink, Andrew chuckled. "Fortunately, I'm able to give the local bakery more and more of my business, buying desserts and speciality breads for the cafe. It's all worked out so much better than I expected. And I have Sean to take over for me, so I can spend more time with Amelia."

"*Ach!* Look at the time. I'm going to be late!" Katie scrambled to her feet, worried about what her boss and her co-workers would think about her tardiness.

"Don't you worry none about that. I'll just be walking you back over to the bakery right now. I need to pick up Amelia anyway. She mentioned having some errands to run this afternoon."

And in no time at all, Andrew was escorting Katie across the street and into the bakery.

three

Anna looked more than a little perturbed when Katie entered the bakery. Most likely she wanted to scold Katie about being late coming back from lunch.

However, when Mr. O'Neal followed Katie into the bakery, Katie thought Anna must have realized what a bad idea it would be and decided to choose her words more carefully.

"Did you have a nice lunch, Katie? You were gone quite a while. We were beginning to wonder if you were coming back at all today."

Katie flushed, but she answered Anna anyway.

"*Jah*, lunch was nice. The food at the cafe is always *gut*. And—"

"Well, I should hope so!" Andrew interrupted. "If that ever changes, you be certain to let me know right away. We can't be feeding our customers food that's not good. What sort of reputation would we get?" Then he winked at the girls.

Just then Amelia came through the doorway.

"Andrew, I was just about to call you. Are you ready to go?"

"Of course I am, Milly. I was just enjoying the company of our wee Katie over at the cafe." Turning to Katie, he continued. "When you have time, I want you to make me some of those orange bliss bars you created. A couple of dozen should be enough for a few days."

"I'll be sure to put them on the list for this afternoon. Travis can bring them over with his late deliveries."

"Nay, Katie-girl. Sometime tomorrow will be soon enough. Doncha be staying late just to make them up today." He gave her his most serious look, before a smile broke out on his face. "Now I want you to promise me you'll wait until tomorrow to do them."

"Andrew, leave the girl alone. She'll make them whenever she has time." Amelia turned to Katie.

"As much as I hate to admit it, Andrew is right, Katie. Don't stay late to finish them today. After all, Andrew's not in a hurry to get them. Please make them whenever you get caught up on your orders for tomorrow."

She turned to head back to her office, then stopped and looked back. "As a matter of fact, go ahead and make up six dozen. It's been a few weeks since anyone has ordered a batch. I'm thinking we should send some over to The Coffee Cup. Mr. Dell and Hannah will enjoy selling them to their customers."

"*Ach*, I forgot to mention what Hannah told me at lunch today." Katie looked stricken. "Oh, but I'm not for sure if I'm supposed to be telling anyone just yet."

"Is this about Charles Dell selling The Coffee Cup and moving away?" Amelia asked.

Katie looked shocked. "*Jah*. You know about it? How did you find out? Mr. Dell just told Hannah this morning. And she just told me at lunch."

Amelia smiled before answering. "Charles Dell and I have known each other for a good many years. Plus, since he decided to buy the breads and desserts that he sells in his cafe from us, we've had several conversations about the future."

"And Charlie and I have had many opportunities to chat lately, too." Andrew interrupted his wife. "He was undecided about what to do after his brother contacted him. He asked me what I would do under the same circumstances. I told him if my family needed me, I would do whatever I could to help. After all, family should come first."

He leaned over to kiss his wife on the cheek before speaking again. "Charlie decided he would feel better about things if he went ahead and sold his house and the cafe and moved in with his brother. He didn't ask me to not say anything. I just figured I wouldn't mention it unless someone asked me about it. Everyone is going to know soon, anyway."

"Charles doesn't have but a few more days until he'll be leaving town. Did Hannah say when the new owner of the cafe would be taking over?" Amelia looked at Katie for her reply.

"*Jah*, he told her his last day to work at the cafe is Friday. She is wondering about all the changes — and when she will meet her new boss. She said it sounded like he would be coming in on Friday. She doesn't expect him any sooner, because Mr. Dell didn't say anything about his coming early. I am for certain thankful that you aren't selling the bakery. I don't want to work for anyone else."

"Don't you worry about that for even a minute, Katie. I have no plans to sell the bakery, or to change anything around here." Amelia reached over to give Katie a hug. "All right, we're going to get going so we can get our errands done and you can get your baking done. I'll see you in the morning."

"Goodbye, Katie-girl." Andrew winked at Katie as he headed toward the door with his wife.

Later in the afternoon, when Travis came in the back door to pick up the orders to be delivered, Katie was hard at work trying to get the day's orders finished. She took a moment to look up, then hurried back to her task.

Seeing no one else in the kitchen, Travis kissed her on the cheek before settling down on a nearby stool.

"How's my best girl doing this afternoon?"

Looking around, he seemed puzzled. "Don't you have any help today? How does Mrs. O'Neal expect you to get all the baking done by yourself?"

"Well, today was a pretty quiet day. And Gwen will be helping me after school."

"Oh, no. Did I forget to tell you this morning? Gwen has a dentist appointment this afternoon. Depending on what he finds, she might not be here at all." Travis sounded upset. "I'm sorry, Katie. I should have remembered to say something to you this morning about it. Then perhaps Mrs. O'Neal could have asked Bella to come in for a few hours at least."

"Bella came in this morning for a couple of hours and she was a big help to me. But right before lunchtime, Mrs. Mueller called to say that Emma was acting cranky and was running a temperature, so Mrs. O'Neal asked me if I could handle things or if Bella could leave early. Of course, I told her I could and to send Bella home to take care of Emma."

"I hope it's nothing serious. I expect Bella or Mrs. Mueller would have let Mrs. O'Neal know if it was." Travis grinned at Katie. "That little girl sure has everyone wrapped around her cute little fingers. But I can't blame anyone. She's the cutest baby I've ever seen."

He leaned in close to whisper in her ear, "Don't tell Thomas or Freida I said that. Their wee babe is a sweetie, too. It's just that Emma seems so full of joy. I don't think I've even seen her cry."

"Bella seems happier now than I've ever seen her, too. I'm glad Mrs. Mueller insisted on them staying with her. Who would have thought? She treats Bella and little Emma like they're family."

"I know. No one would ever have expected it. I guess God really does work miracles." With a chuckle, Travis moved toward the walk-in cooler. "As much as I'd love to stay here with you, I'd better get the deliveries done. But I'll be back as soon as I can."

Travis went back and forth, from the walk-in cooler to the van packed right outside the back door, carefully stowing the orders in the back. When he was finished, he came back in. Walking over to Katie, he pulled her against him.

"Give me a proper goodbye, Katie-girl. I'm gonna be thinking of you while I'm gone." Leaning forward for a kiss, he tried hard not to linger too long. For one thing, he didn't want Anna to catch them kissing. For another, he knew Katie appreciated him not hanging around too long, keeping her from getting her work done.

Keeping Katie happy was important to him; something he always wanted to put before his own goals.

After all, she was worth it.

four

Tuesday morning, Hannah worked hard all morning, while keeping an eye out for Mr. Dell. It was almost lunchtime and so far he hadn't shown up.

The breakfast crowd was over and it was almost time for the lunch rush. Hannah had just brewed a fresh carafe of today's special blend of *kaffe*. While at the serving table, she checked and refilled the containers holding the different varieties of *kaffe* creamers that their regular customers seemed to prefer.

Most of the wooden stirrers had been used during the morning, so she opened a fresh box and replenished the pretty cup that held the stirrers. There was nothing else to do except wipe down the tables.

When the bell over the door jingled, signaling that someone had walked in, she took a moment to give the table she was cleaning an extra swipe before turning around. When she did she found herself staring at a stranger.

"Good morning, sir. How may I help you?"

"And a good morning to you, too. You must be Hannah." The man looked at her as if he knew her.

"*Jah*. I mean, yes." Hannah felt a bit flustered, feeling certain that he was a stranger. If this man knew her, why didn't she remember meeting him? Making the effort to overcome a bit of shyness, she looked at him again. Perhaps the simplest thing would be to ask him.

"Do I know you, sir?"

"Well, no. You don't know me—not yet. But I've heard a lot of wonderful things about you and I've been looking forward to meeting you."

"My goodness! Who has been talking about me?" Hannah couldn't imagine who would be telling things about her to this stranger. She wasn't sure what to think about the situation she had just found herself in.

"I can see you're getting a little upset. Let me assure you, I didn't mean to upset you. Your former boss, Charles Dell, has been telling me all about you." When Hannah slowly backed away from the counter, wondering if she should stay or try to get away from him. the man held up his hands as if he was surrendering and reached toward her.

"Please! It's ok. You see, I'm your new boss. I'm the new owner of The Coffee Cup."

When Hannah threw open the back door of the bakery and burst into the kitchen, Katie was alarmed. Never had Hannah done anything like this before.

"Hannah, is everything okay? What's wrong?"

"Oh Katie, Mr. Dell hasn't shown up yet, but the new owner came in. At least someone who says he's the new owner. But he doesn't look anything like I thought. Nothing like Mr. Dell. This man is very young. Too young to own a business, I think. I was so flustered, I ran out the door and came here as fast as I could."

Katie had never seen Hannah so distressed. Moving quickly, she put her arm around Hannah and led her to one of the nearby stools. Bringing her a glass of water, Katie watched as she took a sip.

"Thanks, Katie. I honestly don't know why I ran out like that. Oh no! I left The Coffee Cup unguarded, with no one there except that man. What must he think? If he's truly the new owner, I probably just lost my job!"

Jumping up, Hannah headed for the door.

"Wait!" Katie called out to her. "Do you want me to go with you? I don't know if it is safe for you to go back alone."

Hannah, who was halfway out the door, stopped and turned around toward Katie. "That would be *wunderbaar*, Katie. Thank you!"

Hurriedly, Katie caught up with Hannah. Reaching out to take her hand, Katie gave it a quick squeeze and they left. Walking back across the street together, they entered The Coffee Cup. A man was standing behind the counter, looking like he wasn't sure what he was doing there... or what he should do next.

"Hannah, thank goodness you came back. Is

something wrong? Where did you go?" The man, whom Katie had figured out must be Hannah's new boss, did not look comfortable at all.

"I'm sorry," Hannah spoke quickly. "I don't know what came over me. I've never done anything like that before."

"I have to say I don't think anyone has ever run away from me before." The man smiled, then spoke again. "And I'm still not sure what I did to provoke such a response."

Hannah blushed a pretty shade of pink. "*Nee*, you did nothing—not really. I just wasn't expecting you today. I didn't think I would be meeting you until Friday. And I was already *naerfich*—I mean nervous—about meeting my new boss. I guess that's you."

Katie thought the more Hannah talked, the more confusing her new boss looked. However, he had the good sense to not move toward her again, but to keep his distance.

"Hello. I am Katie Chupp, Hannah's friend. I

work across the street at The Sweet Shop."

"*Ach*, where are my manners. Katie, let me introduce you to my new boss..."

Hannah stopped, then looked confused. Katie caught a bit of a smile on her lips before she spoke again.

"I'm afraid I cannot properly introduce you. I don't know your name... yet."

Katie and the young man begin laughing. When Hannah joined them, the tension in the air seemed to melt away.

With a slight bow of his head, the man spoke. "Richard Anderson. At your service. You can call me Richard. I am delighted to meet you, Katie. And you, Hannah."

"It's nice to meet you, Richard." Katie was still smiling at the absurdity of their introductions. "Well, Hannah, I guess your new boss has arrived earlier than you expected."

"*Jah*." Hannah replied, then turned to Richard with a look of dread. "And I'm sure I made the worst possible impression on you. But I can assure you, Richard, truly I have never done such a thing before."

"I'm sure you haven't. As a matter of fact, I'm sure I most likely did something to cause it. And really, no harm done. Please don't continue to worry about it."

When Hannah visibly relaxed, Richard continued. "After all, Mr. Dell has assured me that you are completely trustworthy and capable of running the shop all by yourself. I'm looking forward to getting to know you better. And all of our customers, too."

"I don't think I'm needed here any longer, so I'd better be getting back across the street... and back to my baking." Katie waved to them as she opened the door to leave. "Let me know if there's any changes to be made to your order."

After Katie left, Hannah looked around. Since there were no customers at the moment, she thought it would be a good time to show her new boss around the shop. To be sure, she didn't know if he had ever been in The Coffee Cup before. He might have met Mr. Dell here before he had had chosen to buy it.

Still, since she wasn't sure, she decided to go

ahead with her idea to show him the shop as if he had never been there before. Moving around the room, Hannah gave a brief description of each area, then headed to the back of the shop to complete the tour.

"This is where we keep most of the extra supplies. Since I'm usually working by myself, we also keep a few supplies in the cabinets below the counters out front, where it's more convenient if I need to restock an item. Mr. Dell prefers to have extra supplies on hand."

"How often are orders placed for supplies and who normally handles the ordering?"

"We usually place an order every Monday. Mr. Dell used to do all the ordering himself, but for the past few months he's had me do it." Hannah stopped a moment to peer at her new boss. "Will you be wanting to do all the ordering yourself?"

"Well, for now I'd rather leave it to you, as long as you have time to do it. Once I learn the ins and outs of the business, I'd like to take some of the workload off of you so you don't feel over-worked."

"But I don't feel over-worked. Will my job or my hours be changing?"

"No, definitely not. I don't plan to make any changes in your job, or your hours, unless you request a change. I would like to be a part of the day-to-day operations, but that doesn't mean I won't need you to be here. Besides, I'm sure the customers would miss you if you weren't here."

As they walked back to the front of the shop, Hannah looked around at the neat, little tables and chairs before replying.

"I would miss working here, too. I look forward to many of our regular customers who come by at the same time every day and always order the same thing. Even when I suggest a special blend or something Katie has created and sent over, many of them, especially the men, won't order anything but their regular fare."

Hannah's eyes lit up as she thought of how much she enjoyed teasing those who came in. They would laugh and play along, but only a few would ever change their order and try something new.

"Yeah, we men are a bit rigid in our food selections. Especially our coffee. We want what we like... the way we like it."

"Oh, you don't have to tell me. I've been trying for years to get the Mayor to try some of the newer flavored coffees, but he's adamant about drinking the same Columbian coffee with three packets of sugar."

"Does he order a pastry to go with his coffee? Or does he settle for the sugar in his coffee?"

"Well, the Mayor comes in for his coffee every morning, but he also gets coffee and treats for his office workers. More times than not he orders coffee, plus half a dozen of Katie's croissants and a container of cream cheese. I keep a bag made up with sugars and assorted creamers just for him."

"Does he come in every day?"

"Six days a week. Every week. Like clockwork. If we were open on Sundays, he'd probably come in on Sundays, too."

"He certainly sounds like a regular customer. And a nice one, too."

"Oh, he is." Hannah smiled. "We have a lot of nice customers. And we have a few pinheads."

"Pinheads!" Richard burst out laughing, not at all expecting such a word from Hannah.

"Not people in our community; at least, almost none. It's mostly people passing through... people who stop to stare at the strange Amish people."

With a look of distaste, Hannah paused a moment before going on. "They take pictures of us, and ask personal questions. I know I shouldn't let it bother me, but sometimes—"

"I guess I should ask you if you have a problem with having an English boss. I won't ask you any personal questions or take pictures of you. I probably will have lots of questions, but they'll be job-related... or at least related to the community."

"I had't really thought about it before, but I don't think I'll have a problem with an English boss. Mr. Dell isn't Amish and he was a *wunderbaar* boss."

"Yeah, but isn't he Mennonite?" Richard asked. "Isn't his religion very similar to the Amish?"

"Jah, it is somewhat similar, but also very different. We have electricity and use computers only because Mr. Dell is Mennonite and is allowed to have them."

"And I'm thankful for them. I have to say, I would have thought twice about buying The Coffee Cup if it didn't have electricity. And although I could have bought the computer and taught you how to use it, I'm glad you're already up-to-date on it and you don't have any problems using it."

They both turned toward the door when the tiny bell over the door rang as a customer walked in. Hannah excused herself and moved behind the counter to take their order. When another customer entered the store, Richard cleared his throat before speaking.

"I'll be back tomorrow, Hannah." And with a wave goodbye, he left.

five

Wednesday morning, Travis came in the back door of the bakery and looked around, but didn't see anyone—especially the person he was expecting to see.

"Katie, where are you?"

More than a little concerned when he heard no answer, Travis looked for signs of work being done. Aside from a few bowls in one side of the industrial-sized sink, everything looked spotless.

Since it was too early for Mrs. O'Neal to be in

her office, Travis headed toward the front of the bakery.

As soon as he passed through the swinging doors into the main room, he discovered the reason for the workroom to be empty.

Seated at a nearby table was Katie and Amelia, chatting with Ada Mueller, Bella, and little Emma, who was entertaining the others.

When Katie saw him, she looked as if she was going to get up, but her boss put her hand on Katie's arm.

"Katie, stay and enjoy your visit with little Emma. Travis can handle his deliveries without your help."

"I was just going to see if he needed anything before I get back to work."

"Now, dear. You have worked hard this week to keep up with the special orders as well as the regular baking. You deserve a little break... and Emma will be leaving soon with Ada. It'll be time for her nap soon." Amelia looked over at Travis. "Why don't you take a few minutes, too? I bet you haven't seen Emma since she began walking."

"Oh my gosh. Of course I've seen her walking. Little Emma has been walking for a while now." Travis bent down next to the small child, holding his hands out to her. "Hey, Emma. Come give Uncle Trav a big hug."

Katie giggled at the little *maedel*, who was squealing with delight as she toddled over to Travis. A moment later she had leapt into his arms.

The ladies all laughed as Travis noisily kissed her cheeks and tickled her belly, causing her to squeal again. Looking around, he looked puzzled.

"Hey, where's Anna? I didn't see her in the back."

Amelia smiled. "Anna has the morning off. She'll be here this afternoon in time to tend to customers. We'll be fine with Bella here this morning. I don't expect us to be too busy today."

She slowly stood up. "Well, I'm going to go get an early start in the office. Thanks Ada, for walking over with Bella and bringing our precious little girl for a visit." She leaned over and gave the baby several soft kisses on her head, then headed toward her office. Travis and Katie followed her past the swinging doors.

Ada picked up the quilted pink bag, then reached for Emma. "I guess I should be getting this little one home before she starts fussing. Now Bella, don't you worry about this sweet child. She and I will be just fine until you get home."

"No, I won't worry. She loves spending time with you. I'm happy to be able to help out here and earn the money to pay my bills."

"Well, I'm glad to have you and Emma living with me. I don't really need you to continue to pay rent and help with groceries like you've been doing." Ada lowered her voice before going on. "Besides, I thought you told me your parents were sending a check every month to help with your expenses. You could stay home with Emma if you wanted to."

"I know I could. And yes, my parents—although I told them I was doing all right on my own—insisted on helping out financially. But working... well, that's for me. I want to prove to everyone, including me, that I can care of us by myself."

"Then what do you do with your parents' money?" Ada asked, curiosity getting the better of her.

"I'm putting it in the bank each month, to save for the future. I'm hoping I won't need to ever use it. Then it'll be there for Emma. Whether she wants to use it to further her education, or for a big, splashy wedding, or a down payment on a house, it'll be there, waiting for her to do whatever she wants to do with it."

"And what do you think I'm doing with the rent money you give me each month?" Ada asked, with a determined look on her face. "I've been putting it in the bank for a time when you might need it—or Emma might need it. My house is paid for and I get along just fine on my pension. I only take the rent check each month because you insist on it."

"Oh, Ada." Bella ran over to hug the woman who had been more of a mother to her than her own mother had been in years. "Please understand that working—even part time—is important to me. It shows people that I'm taking responsibility not only for my own life, but for my daughter, too."

"Well then, dear. You go ahead and keep working part time. I'll keep watching over this little girl, and everything will work out just fine."

Hugging her friend again, Bella wiped at her eyes. "Whew! I guess I had better get to work then."

She stood at the window, waving at them as they left. After turning over the OPEN sign, she walked behind the counter and pulled her apron from under the counter. As she prepared for her first customer, she silently said a prayer.

Thank you, God, for Ada... and Mr. and Mrs. O'Neal...

and Katie... and everyone in the community that makes me feel like this is home for me—I mean for us. Thank you for guiding me to a place where I finally feel safe and happy. Bless my friends—especially Ada, who has given us such a wonderful home.

Wiping her eyes, she looked up just as the bell over the door rang out the arrival of a customer.

Katie had quickly washed her hands, then started preparing a batch of bread after she went past the swinging doors into the kitchen/work area.

Travis laughed softly. "I guess if you're going back to work, I had better load the morning orders and start my deliveries."

"I guess you better. After taking time off, I'd feel bad if I took another break so soon." Katie giggled. "And maybe if I shoo you out now, you'll be more inclined to meet me for lunch. I was thinking the park would be nice today."

"I don't know, Katie. I might not be able to get away from the cafe. You know Sean depends on me."

"Well, okay—" Before Katie could get out another word, Travis was kissing her soundly.

Quickly ending the kiss, Katie took a deep breath, but stayed wrapped in his arms. "Oh, Travis!"

"I was just teasing you, sweetheart. Of course, I'd love to meet you for lunch. And since I know you don't want your boss to catch us kissing, I'll go now. Once I get my deliveries done, I'll work at the cafe until you can take a lunch break. I'll even fix us a couple of sandwiches, and grab some chips and drinks. How about if you bring the dessert?"

"That sounds *wunderbaar*. I know just what to bring. I worked on a new recipe this morning and you can be my test subject."

"I'll try anything you make, sweetheart. All right, I'm out of here. The fast I work, the faster lunch time will be here. See you in a bit, Katie-girl."

Katie sighed. Her lunch break was almost over. Sometimes it seemed as if the minutes rushed past in a blur whenever she and Travis spent time together.

"What's wrong?" Travis wanted to know.

"Nothing is wrong—exactly. It just seems like we never have enough time when we're together." Katie blushed. "I'm sorry, Travis. I don't mean to complain. It's just... the time goes by so quickly when we're together. I wish I could somehow slow time down when I'm with you."

"Katie, you just said exactly what I feel whenever we're together. I'm thankful for my family, and my friends, and even my jobs. But I wish I had more time to spend with you, too. Every time we're together, I have to stop myself from dwelling on how quickly the time is passing."

"So you think this is pretty normal?"

Travis bent his head near Katie's until they touched. "I don't know if it's normal, because I've never felt this way with anyone else."

"But Travis, you told me about Amber... the girlfriend you had before you moved back to Abbott Creek. You dated her for almost a year, right?"

"Just over a year, until she broke up with me. She said I was too immature and she wanted someone more responsible." Travis looked away.

Katie wondered if he was thinking about how responsible he had become since moving back home.

Is he thinking about trying to get back together with Amber? Am I going to lose him now?

Thoughts ran back and forth through Katie's head, but she remained quietly at Travis' side. Finally she could stand it no longer.

"I guess I had better head back to work." She started to rise, but Travis quickly took her hands in his.

"Sweetheart, you have ten more minutes. You were just saying the time passes too quickly. Surely you don't want to leave early, do you?"

Pulling away from him, Katie stood up. "Bella will be gone and Anna will be there when I return. I'd rather be a little early than give her reason to complain."

She started toward the street, then stopped and looked back. "Thanks for the lunch. I hope you liked the new cookies."

Turning, she practically ran back to the bakery. Travis sat there, watching her until she disappeared.

What just happened? What did I do? And how do I fix it, when I don't know what I've done wrong?

six

Friday morning, Hannah arrived at The Coffee Cup earlier than normal. Mr. Dell had shared that today would be his last day and she wanted to make this day extra special for him.

She began brewing the several varieties of *kaffe* their customers would want, then moved to stock the shelves in the glass case. Once the display case was ready for customers, she replenished the bottles of water and juice in the refrigerated case.

Moving over to the counter space where

customers prepared their coffees, she filled the napkin dispenser. Before she had time to check and refill the various creams and sugars, Mr. Dell was unlocking the door and walking in.

"Good morning, Hannah."

"Good morning, Mr. Dell. How does it feel to be coming in to work for the last time?"

"I thought it would feel good." He moved to pour himself a cup of coffee as he answered her question. "And it does... but it also feels more than a little sad."

Mr. Dell, who had started The Coffee Cup from scratch and enjoyed giving his customers lots of choices of sugars and flavored creams to add to their coffee selection, always drank his coffee black, with nothing added to it. And he always drank the same Columbian roast blend—never anything else.

It tickled Hannah's funny bone to think of how bland their customers would find the owner's own *kaffe* choice. But Mr. Dell always seemed to enjoy his *kaffe* as much as anyone else. Throughout the day, he would refill his cup at least once an hour, and sometimes more often if he was especially busy doing paperwork.

"By the way, Richard should be here soon. He called last night to let me know he'd be here early."

Mr. Dell sat down at a table near the front window. "There are still a few things we need to go over. Do you have any questions for him? Or for me?"

"I don't know. When I met him, he told me things would stay the same for me. I guess one thing I'm curious about is if he wants me to continue as usual and he will take care of the things you've always taken care of, or if he'll be wanting to make some changes."

"Well, then that's one of the things we need to discuss. And I'm not wanting to leave you out of our conversations. You need to speak up whenever you want to or whenever you have a question about anything."

Hearing a noise, they both looked toward the door. A moment later, Richard walked in. Seeing Mr. Dell sitting at a table, he headed over to it.

"Good morning, Charles... and a good morning to you, Hannah." Sitting down, he smiled at Hannah. "Could I have a cup of coffee and a cheese danish, please?"

After watching Hannah a moment, he looked over at the man who would soon be leaving to begin a new life. "Well, Charles. It's your last day. Any regrets?"

"Honestly, the only regret I have is not selling the

cafe sooner and heading to Florida to live with Ben. I don't know why I waited so long to do it. After my wife died, I thought about it—and almost did it."

He paused, looking a bit sad. "But I loved this community. I hated the idea of leaving. And I felt responsible for Hannah, who is the best employee I've ever had. I didn't want to just walk away from it all."

"I can understand that. It sounds pretty normal to me. And Hannah seems like a godsend. I've already gotten the impression that if she needed to, she could run the cafe by herself."

Hannah felt her cheeks getting hot as the blood rushed to her face. Never had anyone spoken of her in such a manner. Surely it was wrong.

"Richard, I fear you've embarrassed Hannah." Charles laughed softly. "She's not used to compliments in this town."

"Well, I call it like I see it—and she's an awesome person, a beautiful young lady and someone I'd really like to get to know better!"

Katie was curious about how Hannah's day was going. She knew it was the last day of work for Mr. Dell. And everyone would want to come by and see him before he left for... oh yeah, Florida. His plan was to move to Florida to live with his brother.

He had told everyone that he was looking forward to doing things with his brother. Plus he was happy that he would be a help to Ben.

And maybe—just maybe—he will find someone special to spend the rest of his days with...

It could happen. It happens every day. And Mr. Dell deserves a happily-ever-after as much as anyone else did. Just look at Mr. and Mrs. O'Neal...

Andrew had been married for nineteen years when his wife Bridget passed away. Then he was alone for seven long years until he met Amelia. It had taken three years to convince her that he was serious about her—and ready for another marriage.

Amelia had been married to Henry for thirty years. After his heart attack, he'd passed quickly. Amelia had thought she would spend the rest of her life alone. This was one reason why she'd opened The Sweet Shop.

Not long after Andrew moved to Abbott Creek, he opened the Irish Blessings Cafe. It was just what the community needed and he enjoyed getting to know his customers, but once he met Amelia, he was determined to win her heart.

But after a misunderstanding, Amelia had left Abbott Creek, with plans to stay away for several weeks. Andrew had tried diligently to find out where she had gone, but no one would tell him. He'd finally persuaded someone—no one knew who it was at the time—to reveal her whereabouts after convincing her that his feelings for Amelia were sincere.

Learning her plans, he'd pursued her all the way to New York, and found her. Ten days later, they returned to Abbott Creek after a wedding cruise and short honeymoon.

Katie thought about Mr. Dell selling his coffee shop and moving to Florida to be close to his brother. She wondered if Mr. Dell would enjoy living with Ben. Would he find things to keep busy?

She couldn't see him becoming a couch potato. Maybe she should talk to Hannah about it. She probably knew more about his plans than anyone else.

Mrs. O'Neal hadn't said anything about the new owner, either. Katie wondered what his plans were for The Coffee Cup. Would she still be baking all of the pastries and desserts Mr. Dell had been ordering from

Mrs. O'Neal for the coffee shop?

Ach, there was no reason to worry about it now. She had plenty to do whether or not she was baking for the coffee shop. Sometimes she wished she had a bit less to do. She loved her job, she truly did, but working full-time, plus Travis working a full-time job at the cafe and still working part-time doing deliveries at the bakery, it was difficult to find time for dating.

And Katie truly enjoyed dating Travis. Most times they didn't plan anything special, just driving to the nearby lake and taking long walks or bringing along a blanket and picnic basket filled with delicious treats, while they talked about their families, their friends, and their future.

Of course, they were both careful discussing the future. There were so many things pulling them in different directions.

Especially Katie's family and church friends, who didn't really approve of Katie dating an *Englischer*. They would prefer she date a nice, Amish boy who would encourage her to be baptized and join the church.

Even more unusual, her *dat* had been insistent on her breaking up with Travis for weeks. Then, just after Bella gave birth to little Emma, her parents sat her down and told her they were fine with her dating Travis. This came as a shock to Katie, who couldn't figure out what had happened to change their minds.

And... there was no more talk about her giving notice and quitting her job. Her *dat* and Bishop Glick had even begun coming by the bakery once or twice a week to get a *kaffe* and pastry.

They would sit at one of the little tables and chat with some of the customers who came in. Whenever Katie could take a break, she'd come out to say hello, but that didn't happen often.

She never felt as if they were checking up on her. It almost seemed as if they were giving Katie—and the bakery—their support. Their approval.

Which didn't make any sense to Katie, since her *dat* had never approved of her working at the bakery. In fact, if Freida Schmidt—now Freida Yoder—hadn't been offered a job at the same time, neither *maedel* would have had a chance to work there.

But the bishop had approved their request since they would be working together. And the only *Englischer* at the times was Mrs. O'Neal, who mostly stayed in her office.

Katie was thankful that neither the bishop, nor her dat, would have guessed that Travis and his *schweschder* would eventually be working there part-time. The biggest challenge was when Katie herself had hired Bella Stanton after she moved to their little town.

Katie had only been able to offer her a temporary position since Mrs. O'Neal was out of town. But Katie had no idea that within a few weeks, Bella would reveal to them that she was pregnant.

A maedel. An Englischer. And pregnant.

When the news came out, Katie felt certain Mrs. O'Neal would be forced to let Bella go when she returned, rather than take a chance that Katie and Freida would have to quit. But quite the contrary.

Instead, Mrs. O'Neal had embraced the young girl and given her a permanent full-time position. Bella was a hard worker and never gave Mrs. O'Neal reason to regret her decision.

Eventually, Bella's story had come out, and the people of Abbott Creek had done all they could to support and help Bella and her child. Katie's own *mamm* had made dozens of baby clothes.

Just before the baby was due, Mr. and Mrs. O'Neal had thrown a huge baby shower and Bella laughed later that there was nothing to buy after the shower, because she had everything she needed.

After Emma was born, Katie's parents had requested that Travis come over for supper once a week so the family could get to know him better—and that his family visit, too, whenever they could. Her family was always welcoming and they seemed to be growing closer to Travis—and his family.

So now, she was dating Travis, with her family's approval and permission. But the future still held the most difficult decisions she had ever made. Would her relationship with him work out?

Katie knew Travis held her heart—and he had told her that she held his, too. But if they married, either he would have to be baptized and give up his *Englischer* ways and live as the Amish, or she would have to choose to not join the church.

Either choice would be one both she and Travis would need to spend much time in prayer over.

seven

Freida came rushing into the bakery. She waved at Anna, but kept going until she reached the kitchen.

"Hey Katie, Thomas and I decided to not wait until Monday, the 30th, to celebrate Tobias' birthday, but to go ahead and have his birthday party next Saturday. I like this idea best. He was born last year on Saturday, and he'll have his birthday this year on Saturday!"

"That's a great idea, Freida." Katie nodded her head as she spoke. "And more people will probably be able to be there on a Saturday. Besides, he's just a baby. He won't know—or care—what day you celebrate his birthday until he gets older."

"That's what I was thinking, too" Freida's excitement was infectious. "Can you please invite Travis and his family? And your family, of course."

"As a matter of fact, Travis and his family are coming to supper tonight, so I can mention it then. What time should we plan to be there?"

"We're telling everyone to come over around four o'clock. Just come on over after you get off work." Freida reached in her pocket for a sheet of paper. "Here's my order for the party. We want to have a small, decorated cake for Tobias to have, plus a full sheet cake for everyone else to enjoy. Or would cupcakes be a better idea?"

"I would do cupcakes, especially if you're planning for a lot of *kinner*. This way everyone can serve themselves. How many people are you expecting? We'll need to know how many cupcakes to make and what icing colors you want on them. And do you have something in mind as far as decorating Tobias' cake?"

"Honestly, I don't know what to ask for. I've seen lots of fancy birthday cakes that you've done, but would it be silly to keep it simple. I for sure don't want him getting too much sugar. We've been so careful for the past year to keep him away from sugar."

"I can't wait to celebrate his very first birthday. And I can do anything you want. A simple cake sounds perfect." Katie took a moment to reach for an order pad and write down all the pertinent information.

"If he's not used to eating sweets," Katie continued, "eating cake and icing, plus ice cream might give him a tummy ache. We for sure don't want that. Why don't you let me surprise you with something simple, but special."

"That sounds perfect." Freida patted her friend's hand. "I knew you'd know just what to do."

"By the way, where is my favorite wee boy today?"

"My *mamm* wanted to keep him at their house while I ran around getting all my errands done. She loves spending time with him and now that he's walking, she's been keeping him outside as much as possible. He loves the kittens and dogs and chickens and goats. Soon enough the weather will change and he'll be stuck inside much of the time."

"*Mamm* says she cannot wait to have wee *boplin* to

spoil. Of course, with none of us married, she has a long time to go before that happens." Katie smiled at the thought of her *mamm* surrounded by little ones. All at once, a tiny *bopli* with Travis' eyes and hair color popped up in her thoughts.

Ach, I shouldn't be thinking of that now... not until I'm more sure in my heart what the right thing is to do—and for sure, whatever decision I make will effect my family and friends. Why is lieb so complicated...

She sighed, then turned back to her friend. "*Allrecht*, what's next of your list of things to get done today?"

Freida glanced at the sheet of paper in her hands. "I guess next thing to do is put a sign in the window. Mrs. O'Neal suggested leaving signs around town."

"That will work out for all the *Englischers* in town." Katie chuckled. "Of course, the word will pass around on Sunday until most everyone will hear about it."

"*Jah*, you're right about that." Freida giggled. "Well, I guess the next stop should be The Coffee Cup. I was planning to go by anyway to say goodbye to Mr. Dell—and meet the new owner, if he's there."

"Hannah says Mr. Dell plans to stay the whole day, hoping to see as many friends as possible before he leaves. You know he's planning to head out first thing in the morning."

"I heard he was going to be at the shop all day. Thomas and I weren't certain if he would leave tomorrow or wait until Sunday. That makes sense — to go ahead and leave tomorrow." Freida looked a little sad.

Katie knew her her friend would miss Mr. Dell. She would miss him, as well. They had both known him pretty much all their lives.

"*Ach*, well I guess I'll be heading over there now. I'll see you at church on Sunday, Katie."

"Bye, Frieda." As Freida stepped outside, Katie headed toward the kitchen. There was still lots to be done and she was planning to go back over to visit with Mr. Dell after her work was done.

When Freida entered The Coffee Cup, the room was more crowded than she had ever seen it. Mr. Dell was sitting at a table next to a window. Joining him was a younger man she had never seen before.

But even more unusual, Bishop Glick and Mayor Robertson were sitting with him, and chatting with everyone who stopped at the table to say their goodbyes and wish him well.

Joining Hannah behind the counter, was Travis Davis and his *schweschder* Gwen, wearing aprons, and working diligently to keep the long line moving. It looked as if most of the glass case was empty of pastries. Hannah looked flustered, but kept a smile on her face.

While she watched, Hannah hurried over to brew more *kaffe*. Although most everything had already sold out, customers smiled and chatted, waiting their turn to talk to Mr. Dell.

Obviously, they weren't there to fill their tummies, but to shake Mr. Dell's hand or give him a hug, as they reassured him he would be missed—and welcomed back anytime he could visit.

Bishop Glick motioned Freida over to their table. Mr. Dell stood, but before he could move to shake her hand, Freida put one arm around him and gave him a hug.

"Mr. Dell, I am really going to miss you. But I know you're happy to be going to spend time with your *bruder*, and I hope you and he have many special times. Don't forget to take him to Sarasota. Pinecraft is a popular place, too. The best time to visit is in the winter. It's the place to go if you need to get away from the cold."

"That's just the place Bishop Glick has been telling me about." Mr. Dell sat back down before he continued.

"He's been saying that he and Mary might just make a visit in January and they'll make sure Ben and I have a place to stay with them if we decide to drive up. I tell you what, it's certainly tempting. I think I'll mention it to Ben the first chance I get and we can make plans to go."

The younger man sitting with Mr. Dell had excused himself and headed to the storeroom in the back. After saying goodbye to Mr. Dell, the bishop, the mayor, and waving to Hannah and the others, Freida followed a group of people out.

She turned toward the Irish Blessings Cafe. Mr. O'Neal had promised to put a sign in his window telling the community about the birthday party the following week. Then she needed to pick up Tobias and head home to start supper for her starving husband.

"*Mamm*, I'm back." As Freida closed the door behind her, Tobias squealed and pulled himself up to hurry over to her. He grabbed hold of her skirt and tried to climb up. She quickly picked him up and tickled his tummy before giving him a hug. "Were you a good *buwe*, Toby?"

Sarah Schmidt stood watching them a moment, before crossing the room to hug her *dochder*. "*Ach*, the little scamp got into the flour and made a mess on the floor. But it's not his fault."

She leaned over to rub her hand over Tobias' hair. "It was your *dat's* fault. He left the bag on the floor last night. I meant to put it up on a shelf today, but Tobias got to it first. So the kitchen got a *gut* cleaning and then Tobias got a bath."

Laughing, Freida gently patted his bottom. "Tobias Yoder! You for sure keep *Mamm* busy as a bee whenever you visit."

"He's no trouble and you know it. I love having him over. And I could do with several more. So when is he getting a little *bruder* or *schweschder*?"

"Now *Mamm*, you know Thomas and I need to

finish the house we're building before that happens. As it is, Thomas and Timothy are working on it most every weekend. We're hoping it's ready to move into sometime this winter" Freida stopped, looking unsure if she should say more. She decided to mention Thomas' *bruder*.

"And it's not going any faster since Timothy decided all of a sudden to start working on his own house. Why he needs his own house when he's not even dating, I don't know. But he says he's determined to get his done before Christmas—and he assured Thomas that our house will be ready by then, too."

"That's *wunderbaar*, dear. I'm sure you'll be happy to finally be in your own house, although you made a fine home in the Yoder's *daudi* house after you and Thomas married."

"For sure, we're both looking forward to it." Freida leaned closer to whisper to her mom. "And Christmas is the best time for surprises... and announcements."

Freida winked at her mom, then she turned and left.

eight

After Katie finished her work and the bakery was clean, she headed across the street. Entering the coffee shop wasn't easy; there were people everywhere.

She decided to let everyone else enjoy his last time at the shop, so she got as close as she could, then waved to get his attention.

"Mr. Dell, It has been an honor knowing you. I just wanted to say goodbye and wish you the best in the future." With a smile, she quickly left the shop before she allowed her emotions to get the best of her.

Travis had only seen Katie twice today. Both times she was so busy, he felt badly about interrupting her, so he didn't stop and talk to her. He was thinking once she left the bakery, he could spend some time with her.

Then while he was working his full-time job at the Irish Blessings cafe, Mr. O'Neal had come out to the kitchen to mention how terribly busy Hannah was at The Coffee Cup, and Travis had volunteered to run over and help out. Once he arrived, he saw his little sister standing behind the counter with Hannah, putting on an apron.

"Hey, Gwen. What are you doing here?"

"Mrs. O'Neal asked if I would come over to help Hannah, and of course I said I would. When I got here it was so busy, I was really glad I did. I asked Hannah to let me know what she needed me to do."

"First, she asked me to clean up a little," she said. "Then she asked me to put on an apron and help her behind the counter. That's what I was just doing—getting ready to help her behind the counter. So what are you doing here?"

Travis laughed. "Well, that's what I'm doing, too. Mr. O'Neal asked if anyone would help out here. When I volunteered, he sent me over and told me to stay as long as Hannah needs me. Hand me an apron, please. Then we'll get busy and take care of all these customers."

Hannah, Gwen, and Travis quickly cleaned up the shop. With the extra help, it didn't take long until all the pastries, breads, and most of the drinks were sold out. People coming in didn't seem to mind. They had come by mainly to say their goodbyes to Mr. Dell.

Richard, the new owner, came over to say that Mr. Dell was nearly ready to leave. For now, he was heading outside to chat with anyone else coming by and he had suggested that Hannah and her helpers go ahead and close the shop.

"Hannah, you did an amazing job today. I hope all this extra work didn't put you off. Please come back tomorrow. I'll be in early and will help you any way I can. You don't need to worry about doing everything yourself."

"Of course I'll be back tomorrow, Mr. Anderson. I am thinking that as soon as the bakery opens, I should run over to pick up any pastries and breads that are available, so I can come back and fill as much of the case that I can."

"That sounds fine. You do that. I've already let Amelia know that today we sold out of what we had available. She says it won't be a problem to help fill the case, and she's contacted her part-time help to come in as early as they can to help Katie with the baking.

"Oh, that's *gut*. I'm sure everything will be okay."

"Now you and your friends go ahead and leave. And you get plenty of rest tonight. You deserve it and I'm certain you need it. Good night."

But of course, before she left, Hannah had to give Mr. Dell a goodbye hug.

"Please let me know how you and your *bruder* are making out. And thank you again for all you've done for me."

"You're most welcome, Hannah. I'll be sure and call to let you know once I get to my brother's home. And now it's time for us to leave. Goodbye, my dear."

And with one last hug, Mr. Dell turned and left.

After the supper dishes were done, Katie went outside to sit on the porch steps. She knew Mrs. O'Neal had asked Gwen to go to the coffee shop to help Hannah. When she stepped in to see Mr. Dell one last time, she noticed Travis was helping and figured Mr. O'Neal had asked for his help, too.

But she wasn't sure why Travis hadn't even spoken to her the two times he came into the kitchen of the bakery to pick up orders to be delivered.

She was certain she hadn't said or done anything to annoy or upset him. It wasn't often that she fretted over their relationship.

Perhaps it was because her emotions were already engaged. Mr. Dell had been a part of her community as long as she could remember. She was going to miss, for sure and for certain.

However, his decision seemed like a *gut* one—for him, as well as for his *bruder*. She had wished him the best, and she meant it.

A few minutes later, her *dat* and *mamm* came outside. They headed for the porch swing. Sitting down, they looked over at Katie, then her *dat* spoke.

"Katie, where is your young man tonight? Not that we're complaining, mind you. It's nice sitting out here with our oldest *dochder* on such a nice night."

"I don't know where he is tonight, *Dat*. I saw him and his *schweschder* at The Coffee Cup when I went over to say goodbye to Mr. Dell. They were helping out behind the counter. But I'm for sure they've left by now. They probably headed home to have supper with their family."

"I'm certain Charlie Dell is going to enjoy retiring and spending more time with his *bruder*. He always found the time to visit him every year, but I hear his *bruder* has health issues and needs a bit more help now. Charlie is for sure an answer to his *bruder's* prayers."

Caleb looked thoughtful. "I am blessed with this family—and this community. And even more blessed with good health."

Martha leaned over against her husband. "And

we are blessed with such a *wunderbaar* husband, and *dat*, and community leader."

After her parents went inside, Katie moved from the porch step to the swing. Gently swinging, with a cool breeze and the sound of crickets chirping, Katie tried to clear her mind and relax.

Hearing the sound of a familiar car, Katie watched as Travis pulled up the drive. Getting out, he saw Katie on the porch and headed over to her. Sitting down next to her, he took her hand in his, then bent over to gently kiss her cheek.

"Hiya, Katie-girl. I missed you today."

"You did?"

"Yeah, I did. I saw you when I came in to pick up the orders, but you looked so busy, I hated disturbing you. I was hoping if I left you to do your work, you would maybe finish early and we could go for a drive. I had no idea that Mr. O'Neal would ask if someone could help out at The Coffee Cup."

"I noticed you there when I came in after work,

but you look busy so I spoke to Mr. Dell and then left."

"I never even saw you come in... that's how busy we were. Gwen was a huge help, too. She told me Mrs. O'Neal had asked her to help out, too. Once we were done, she was so tired, I just drove on home so we could get something to eat. But I couldn't go to bed without seeing you."

He stopped a moment, as if to gather his thoughts, before speaking again. "I could be wrong. I hope I am. But it seemed to me that you got upset over something a few days ago."

"No, I cannot think of anything."

"Sweetheart, it's not like you to run away. Especially when you've just mentioned wishing we had more time to spend together. Please tell me what I did—or said—so I can fix it."

"Travis, it's truly nothing."

"Now Katie, if you don't tell me, I won't be able to fix it. Please tell me."

"If you must know, I got to wondering about our relationship, and if something—or someone—could cause you to have second thoughts about being a boyfriend to someone with so many difficult decisions that will affect our relationship—both right now and in the future. I was wondering about Amber and if you and she might be ready to try again."

Travis stopped the gentle moving of the swing. Slightly turning in his seat, he took both her hands in his. "Katie, my dearest love, you never, never, ever, need to worry about Amber—or anyone else in my past, present or future, taking your place in my heart."

Katie was shocked to see a tear moving down his cheek as he spoke again. "Don't you know how much I love you? I would do anything... anything... for you."

"Just say the word and I will talk to your bishop about being baptized and joining your church." He cleared this throat before speaking again. "I will give up everything and live the rest of my life as a Godly, Amish *mann* to you and *dat* to our *kinner*."

His voice shook a little as he continued. "I know your church is important to you and I will happily leave mine and join yours—if you tell me that's what you need. Never doubt my love for you again, dearest."

"I am ready—right now—to make you a part of my life—and be a part of yours. Permanently." He cleared his throat again, then took a couple of deep breaths, before going on.

"I haven't wanted to rush you, so I've waited for a sign... a word... something from you that would show me that you're ready for me to take the next step. Are you ready now? Are you ready to give me an answer to the most important question I'll ever have the honor to ask you?"

"I don't know, Travis. I truly don't know." Katie looked stricken. "*Ach*, not about loving you. I know that I love you—and only you. A forever love. And I know what I want my answer to be when you ask me that question."

She stopped for a moment before speaking again. "But I want to be certain before joining the church—or leaving the church. I never want to question my decision in the future. I want to be one hundred percent sure and never doubt the decision once I make it."

"Then where does that take us?"

"The church is the only thing standing in the way. Can you—will you—give me the time I need to be certain of what to do, which road to take?"

"Yes! Of course I will." Travis pulled her to him, hugging her tightly. "Now may I please have a kiss?"

Katie pulled his head down to hers, and when their lips joined, Travis felt as if he was experiencing a little bit of heaven on earth.

However, he made certain he remembered where they were. He wasn't about to do anything to upset Katie's parents. Pulling back just a little, he allowed himself to enjoy a few more kisses, keeping them as chaste as possible.

Then he brushed her hair back, and placed a gentle kiss on her nose. "All right, sweetheart. Let's not upset your parents. I'll be back in the morning to drive you to work. I'd like to take you home with me tomorrow for supper, if that's okay.

"That sounds nice. I love visiting your family. I'll plan a dessert to bring."

"Then I'll go now, and I'll be back in the morning. Good night, sweetheart."

"Good night."

nine

Saturday morning at The Coffee Cup began as usual. Just like always, Hannah arrived promptly at five thirty A.M. to give herself thirty minutes to prep the shop and brew the *appeditlich kaffees* they sold to customers.

Nonetheless, there was a definite change in the air. Last night Mr. Dell had said his last goodbyes to most everyone in the community, then spent a few minutes wishing Hannah and the new owner, Richard Anderson, the very best. After he left, Richard told

Hannah she should go ahead and leave and he would close up.

Hannah had just began restocking the shelves when Richard showed up.

"Good morning, Hannah. I thought I'd come in early and see what's involved in getting the shop ready for customers. Charles said you rarely ever take a day off, but I should probably learn how, just in case something comes up and you need to miss work."

"Good morning, Mr. Anderson. I don't expect to be taking time off anytime soon, but being the new owner, that does sound like a *gut* idea."

"By the way, I would much prefer it if you would call me Richard, or Rick."

"*Ach*, I'm not sure how comfortable I feel using your first name, since you're my boss. Mr. Dell told me when he gave me the job that I could call him Charles, but I could never bring myself to do it. Even though our Amish church is one where we use first names and not surnames, work seems different. I would rather continue to call you Mr. Anderson."

"And I would rather you call me Richard. I've heard your friends refer to Andrew and Amelia as Mr. and Mrs. O'Neal, but I'm much younger than they are and I want you to call me Richard. Please do this for me. Otherwise I'm going to feel much older... and I'll feel like I don't really fit in here."

"Well, if you insist, I'll try. I really will."

"And now let's get to work. I don't want to slow you down and it's almost time to open the shop."

"You're amazing!" Richard told Hannah as they were cleaning up after the shop closed.

"*Danki*, Mr. Anderson," Hannah blushed as she looked pleased, but a little embarrassed. "I'm just doing what I always do."

"Living in a big city for years has made me wonder if anyone really cares about doing a good job anymore. You've restored my faith in people. You really care about doing a good job... and you care about all the customers, too." He paused a moment, then gave her a smile. "And it's Richard, not Mr. Anderson. You make me feel like the bad guy in a movie I used to watch when you call me Mr. Anderson."

To his surprise, Hannah burst out laughing. "I'm

sorry. It's just so strange to picture you as a bad guy. You are nothing like a bad guy. You are so much nicer to work for than I expected."

"Then I guess I can expect to hear you calling me Richard from now on. Hmm?"

"I will do my best, Richard."

"That sounds good. Now let's get done and go home."

Katie was having a wonderful time with the Davis family. After a delicious supper of meatloaf, mashed potatoes and sweet peas, Katie brought out the iced lemon bar cake she had prepared earlier. Soon there was nothing left but a few crumbs.

Sam and Trevor, Travis' younger brothers, didn't complain when their mom asked them to clear the table, then to wash and put away the dishes. While they were busy in the kitchen, Cissy asked Travis and Katie how their day was and if Mr. Dell had left on his journey to Florida on time.

"Actually, Mr. Dell came by just after I arrived to

leave his house keys for Mrs. O'Neal, then he left. She'll pass them along to the real estate agent on Monday so his house can be shown to prospective buyers." Katie shared

"How did you do it?" Travis teased Katie.

"Honestly, I have no idea. All this time I kept forgetting and calling him Bobby. Last night, for some reason, I finally remembered to call him Bob, and what did he do? He — "

"He surprised everyone by saying he no longer wanted to be called Bob and from now on would we please just go back to calling him Bobby!" Travis chuckled when Katie broke down in giggles. "Sam and Trevor took great delight calling him Bob over and over again last night before he went to bed."

"I'm sure they enjoyed it, too. That's just what my own *bruders* would do. Thankfully, most Amish *kinner* are always called by their given names."

Travis took her hand as they drove toward her home. "Did you have a *gut* time tonight, Katie?"

"*Jah*, I had a very *gut* time. I love my *mamm's* cooking, but there's something special about your *mamm's* cooking, too. I feel like part of your family when I'm there—and I like that feeling a lot."

"I like that feeling, too. And I like that you are the only girl I've ever brought home to meet my family. It seems to make every visit special."

"*Danki* for telling me that. I guess you know you're the only *buwe* I've invited home to meet my family. *Ach*, there's been more than a few that have come for supper that are friends of my bruders, but I was never interested in any of them."

"I must confess I have wondered, since it seems like your brothers are always having friends over. And I wouldn't blame them if they were all trying to gain your attention. But if you say you were never interested in any of them, I know you're being truthful and there's nothing for me to worry over."

"There's only one *buwe* I have ever been interested in—and I tried hard not to be, with him being an *Englischer* and all, but I just couldn't help myself."

Travis squeezed her hand, then pulled it toward him until he could hold it against his heart.

"I love you, Katie."

"And I love you, Travis."

Andrew O'Neal watched as his wife got ready for bed. Once she had hung her robe on a hook, he waited patiently for her to join him. After they'd returned from their honeymoon, Andrew had agreed to move into her house.

He had moved his clothes to the walk-in closet in their bedroom, then a few days later he had brought over his personal items, a few pictures, and several boxes of books.

Amelia had been comfortable using her full-size bed that she had brought to Abbott Creek, along with the rest of her furniture. The only change Andrew requested when he moved in was that they purchase a queen-size bed with a new pillow-top mattress and box springs.

They both had agreed that a queen-size bed was the perfect size for them. It was close enough for cuddling,which Andrew insisted was necessary. And it was also wide enough for a bit of space when sleeping.

"Come closer, love. You're much too far away."

"Andy, you're just plain silly."

"Silly or not, I want you closer, woman. Now scoot—or do I have to come get you and carry you to bed!"

"All right, dearest. You know very well how I love snuggling with you, although I admit I've worried a bit that you would soon tire of me and want more space."

As Amelia scooted over until Andrew could wrap an arm around her, she giggled. "Do you realize we've almost been married for a whole year?"

"Impossible! It seems like yesterday that I was flying to New York, hoping and praying that I'd arrive in time to catch you before you sailed the seas."

"And you caught me—and had your Irish way with me." She giggled again. "And I'm so glad you did. But we're about to celebrate a year of married life."

"Nay, it cannot be almost a year. It's still so new."

"I have to admit, most of the time you behave like we're still newlyweds. Let me be clear... I am not complaining. Not in the least. On the contrary... I am thrilled to see you behave as one. Don't stop."

He only smiled and tucked her a bit closer.

"But, sweetheart, about our anniversary, is there

something special you want to do to celebrate? You know I would do anything for you."

"I can't think of anything I'd rather do than spend the day with you, here in our home, with maybe a short visit with wee little Emma."

"Done. I love that you want to spend the day at home with me."

He smiled again. "But... I want you to be thinking about visiting Ireland for our fifth anniversary. Perhaps we can take Sean with us. We'll introduce you to family and friends who are still living there."

"Oh Andy! I don't have to think about it at all. That sounds like a great idea."

"Ah, tis a grand thing. Then I'll start making plans. I only have four years but I do think I can be ready."

He chuckled, pulling her closer. He kissed her again, thankful that he had wooed and finally won her. "Now, come snuggle with your old husband and let's talk about love..."

Hannah lay in her bed, thinking about how different it felt working at The Coffee Cup. Mr. O'Neal had come in just before the coffee shop closed to let Hannah and Richard Anderson know that Charles Dell had reached the halfway point and was stopping for the night.

When planning his trip, Mr. Dell had decided to stop in Indian Springs, Georgia. He had figured it would take him about ten hours, including a couple of stops, to reach the hotel he had booked for the night.

The next morning, after eating a hearty breakfast, he would fill up the fuel tank, check the oil, and get back on the road. This way he would arrive at his brother's house sometime Sunday evening.

Several men in the community had suggested he take a break on Sunday, and after talking with them, he agreed. Sunday afternoon he planned to drive to the Indian Springs State Park, one of the oldest state parks in the United States.

After another night to rest, Charles was determined to get an early start and make it to his *bruder's* house by Monday evening.

Hannah was very happy for her previous boss, but she was going to miss him... and it was going to take some time to get used to Mr. Anderson—oops, she had promised to call him Richard.

So far, everything was working out. Thankful that tomorrow was Sunday and she could rest after church and the lunch afterwards, she took time for prayer, then closed her eyes, hoping sleep would come quickly.

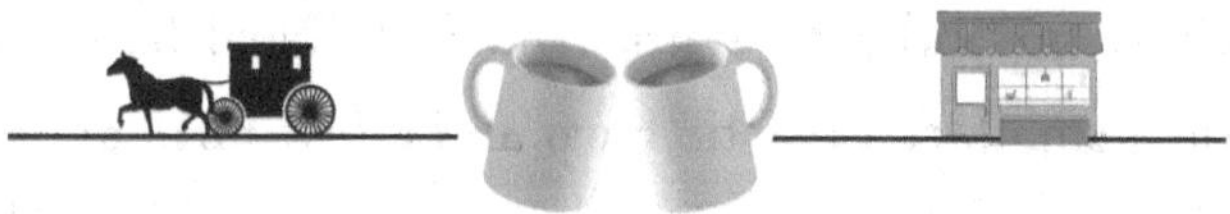

ten

Freida and Thomas Yoder were happily getting ready to celebrate their son's first birthday. Tobias would turn one on September 30th, but since he was born on a Saturday, Freida wanted to celebrate his first birthday today—Saturday, September the 28th.

Pretty much everyone had been invited to the gathering. Freida, her *mamm*, and Katie had all been preparing for a big crowd, and everything was ready.

Travis had driven Katie and Gwen over early so Katie would have time to lay out the cupcakes she had made for everyone, plus a special cake she had fussed over—just for Tobias.

The cake and icing were white, which would please Freida, who didn't want Tobias to be tasting the dyes that color the icing. But she didn't object to just a little color, so Katie used a pale green frosting to write Tobias' name on the cake.

After making sure that they were safe for babies to chew on and play with, Amelia O'Neal had given Katie a small, red plastic barn and a few farm animals to place atop the cake. Freida actually squealed when she saw it.

"Ach, it's wunderbaar, Katie. Danki for the wondrous cake. For sure, Tobias will enjoy the barn and animals."

"You can thank Mrs. O'Neal for the toys. She wanted something that was safe, but would remind you and Thomas of your baby's very first birthday. They are very well made, so they should last a *gut*, long time."

Freida put the small cake away in a cabinet to hide it until it was time to give it to Tobias. By the time Katie had the cupcakes arranged on the table laden with bowls and plates of finger foods for the guests, several buggies had turned in at the drive and were heading toward the nearby barn, where the horses would be given water and hay. There they would rest until it was time to return to their homes.

After the party ended, most of the women helped Freida with the cleanup. It didn't take long with everyone helping. Soon enough, buggies were lined up in the gravel driveway, making their way to the road.

After the buggies were gone, Freida and Thomas watched Travis and Katie drive away in his car. Travis' mother and siblings had ridden home in Andrew's big truck. He and Amelia had been invited to the Davis home for supper and were looking forward to the visit.

Travis and Katie made their excuses, saying they had made other plans. They were heading to their favorite pizza restaurant. Of course, they hadn't said anything about where they were going, or his brothers would have begged to go with them.

Even though Travis usually brought pizza home to share with his family on Sunday afternoon so his mom wouldn't have to cook, the boys loved pizza so much they would eat it every day if it was available.

But tonight was a date night, meaning Travis and Katie were able to spend time together as a couple. They tried to have a date every week, but much too often there was extra work to be done or something else would come up, causing them to cancel their date night.

Freida had invited Katie to use their bedroom to change clothes for her date. Thomas had suggested that Travis wait until the Amish families had left before pulling his car up to the *daudi* house to pick up Katie.

Katie's parents knew she wore *Englischer* clothes sometimes on her dates with Travis, but it just made sense to not draw attention to her choice of clothing to those in her church.

Driving toward the pizza parlor, Travis smiled. "Did you enjoy the birthday party, Katie?"

"*Jah,* it was fun. I think everyone had a *gut* time.

Especially little Tobias. After opening the first gift, he was so cute about hanging on to it. He didn't care about the others. He just wanted to play with the one he had." She giggled before going on. "I think it was *gut* that no one fussed about him not opening the others. I wonder how many days it'll take before he opens them all?"

Travis laughed with her as they pictured the little *buwe* holding tightly to the toy when the others tried to take it and give him another one.

"I think it might take a week or more. But that will just make the birthday last longer, won't it?"

"*Jah*, I like that idea."

"Just don't remind Bobby, or he'll want his birthday to last a week or more." They both laughed again.

Parking his car, Travis walked around to open Katie's door and help her out. As he let go of her hand, he leaned in and pulled her close for a hug.

"Sweetheart, did I say how nice you're looking tonight? I really like the yellow shirt you're wearing. And you always look great wearing Bella's jeans."

"Actually, these are my own jeans. I went shopping and bought jeans, tops, and a couple of sweaters. So what I'm wearing tonight are some of my new clothes."

"Well, the yellow shirt reminds me of sunlight. It's a great color on you because you definitely brighten up my days."

After a couple of chaste kisses, he put his arm around her. "I think we should go have some of that delicious pizza before someone notices us smooching."

Katie giggled. "Smooching! That's what my *dat* calls it." Thinking of it, she giggled again.

"Well, I can assure you I didn't pick up the term from your *dat*. I don't think your *dat* wants to talk to me about smooching his *dochder*. Nope. He might want to talk to me about NOT smooching his *dochder*."

Katie was still laughing as Travis held the door for her. Once inside, they quickly chose a place to sit. Travis went to the counter to place their order and pay for their food, then he returned to the table with two soft drinks. He sat down and said a quick prayer for the food, then added a silent prayer, thanking God for such a wonderful girl as Katie, to be his girlfriend.

Something had woken Thomas Yoder, although the small house they lived in was quiet. When he realized his *frau* wasn't lying beside him, he sat up in bed and looked over at the rocker, where Freida was gently rocking while feeding young Tobias.

"Did we wake you? I tried to get him before he started crying so you could sleep."

"*Nee*, he didn't wake me. I woke and missed your presence, that's all. I love watching you feed our son. You are a *wunderbaar mamm*."

"I've been meaning to talk to you about something, but we've both been so busy this week there never seemed to be a *gut* time."

"*Was iss letz?* You can talk to me now."

"Nothing is wrong. Something is *gut*. Something is *wunderbaar*!" Freida took a deep breath before going on. "We're gonna have another *bopli*..."

Thomas jumped up from the bed and hurried to the rocker, where he sank to his knees and wrapped his arms around her and the *bopli*—both *boplin*.

"That's the best news I've had since you told me the news that we were expecting Tobias."

"Oh, Thomas, I'm so happy. Just so happy. Now Tobias will have a little *bruder* or *schweschder*."

"I cannot wait to tell my *mamm*. Have you told

your *mamm* yet?"

"*Nee*, Thomas. I haven't even told Katie—my best friend. I wanted you to be the first to know, just like last time. You are the most *wunderbaar* husband and you will always be first in my heart—except for *Gott*."

"As it should be, my lovely *frau. Gott* gave me a enormous blessing when he gave you to me."

"I feel the same about you, my strong, handsome husband."

"Sweetheart, when do you expect this *bopli* to come?"

"The best I can figure, using my last period, is the end of May of next year. Do you think our house will be finished and we can be moved in by then?"

"Oh *jah*, I'll make sure that it's ready. I'll talk to Timothy and *Dat* about getting some help so we can move in sooner. When they hear about the new *bopli*, everyone will help us get moved quicker than we planned."

"Oh Thomas, that's something else I wanted to talk to you. Do you mind if we keep the news to ourselves for a while? I was thinking about telling Katie in a few weeks but waiting and surprising everyone at Christmas. That will be such *gut* Christmas news."

"Sure, whatever you want to do. I'm gonna ask Travis to help me build another chicken coop. The chickens we have now are *gut* egg producers, and the roosters make *gut* fryers. I think we could handle more."

"Whatever you think is fine. Tobias is sleeping so I'm gonna put him back in his bed and try to get a little more sleep."

When Freida lay down beside her husband, the first thing he did was give her another hug, and a warm, sweet kiss. Freida loved his kisses. They always reminded her of Christmas time.

Thomas and his *bruder* always carried peppermints in their pockets. His kisses were sweet like peppermints. She expected Timothy's did, too.

Thomas and Freida spent several minutes sharing warm, sweet kisses, before he pulled her over to lie close to him. It didn't take long for them to fall asleep.

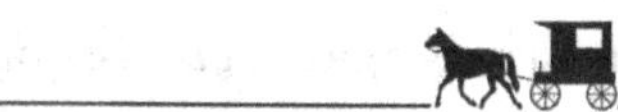

Caleb and Martha Chupp were lying in bed, but neither one of them had fallen asleep. Although they both had to get up early every day, it was near impossible for them to stop thinking about their *dochder* being out on a date with Travis Davis, instead of in her bed asleep.

To be sure, Travis usually brought Katie home at a reasonable hour, but Caleb still couldn't get to sleep until he knew she was home. Since the day she was born, her *dat* had felt just a bit over-protective of her.

When Leah and Dora joined the family, Caleb had felt just as protective of them. He had taught his three *buwes* to be strong, hard-working and to always watch over their three *schweschders*.

Now, he was fearing that he was about to lose one of his girls. After he learned of Bella's past, he and Martha had went to the bishop to see if he had heard of her situation.

Learning that the bishop's *frau* Mary had shared the news with him, Caleb told him that Katie was resistant about being baptized and joining the church. He also told him that she was dating a young, *Englischer buwe*, but that Travis was a *gut* young man, and that he always showed her great respect and was a big help not only to his family, but to several Amish families in their community.

The bishop asked if his *frau* could join them.

When she did, she shared that she and Katie had talked about her choices during *rumschpringe* and that she had advised Katie to be sure about her decision regarding the church. She had also told Katie that they would rather Katie not join the church if she wasn't certain of her future, because she would still be welcome among their people unless she joined the church, then chose to leave it.

The bishop had told Caleb and Martha that he supported his *frau's* advice to Katie, and if she chose a life with Travis, and didn't join the church, that *Gott* — and the church — would still be a big part of her life, and her family should consider it a blessing that she could still be welcomed at her family's home, and the church.

Caleb and Martha had returned home, determined to support Katie in whatever decision she made. They agreed that she was a blessing, whether she joined the church or married Travis, and they prayed that she would never be exposed to such a horror as what had happened to Bella.

Hearing a car engine running, then silence, assured them that their *dochder* was safely home.

"Now I can get to sleep." And within minutes, he was.

Martha grinned at the sound of her husband snoring lightly, then almost as quickly she too, fell asleep.

Travis helped Katie out of the car, then led her to the porch swing, where they usually spent a few minutes, gently swinging while they were kissing.

The next day was an off Sunday, so Katie had agreed to go to his church with his family. Sometimes it was very difficult to stop kissing his adorable girlfriend, but he wanted to protect her—even from himself—so he did his best to maintain a strict control over the situation, especially when they were alone.

He had quickly learned that it was easiest to stop kissing when it began to get intense, just by pulling her head down on his shoulder, then taking her hand and holding it while swinging slowly.

He also tried not to keep her out late, nor to hug and kiss too long, because he wanted her *dat* to trust him, and see that he was being respectful of her.

"Katie, I guess it's time for me to go. But I'll be

back in the morning to pick you up, if you still want to visit our church tomorrow."

"*Jah*, I still want to go."

"Okay then, one more kiss and then off you go to bed and get some sleep. I'm really looking forward to sitting with you at my church, and introducing you to the pastor and his wife."

He smacked his head. "Oh, I forgot to tell you. You're also invited to lunch, too. Our church is having a fellowship lunch right after church and maybe I can introduce you to some of the friends we've made there."

Travis looked a little unsure of himself. "That is, if you'd like to meet them."

"I think I would like to meet all your friends, and your pastor. Tomorrow sounds like a lot of fun. I can't wait!"

She stood up, then waited for Travis to get to his feet. Then she leaned toward him, and kissed him gently on the lips. Ending the kiss, she put her arms around his middle and hugged him. He hugged her back, feeling truly blessed.

He waited until she had walked inside and closed the door, then he walked back to his car, and sat for several minutes, just thinking of how he loved his sweet Katie. Then he headed home.

eleven

The next morning, Katie talked to her *mamm* about what would be appropriate to wear to a baptist church. While Martha would rather Katie always wear her Amish clothes, she admitted to herself that Katie might have an easier time if she wore *Englischer* clothing.

When Katie sought her out to ask if she would be upset if she didn't dress in her Amish garb, Martha was ready with her answer.

"As much as I prefer your own clothes, perhaps it would be better, if you have some plain, *Englischer* clothes, that you dress as they do. This way, you'll not look out of place, and Travis or his family won't get asked a lot of questions about why you're there today if you're of the Amish faith."

"*Danki, mamm.* I do have a dress I can wear. It's plain, but I think it's pretty. And you're right. I'll fit in much better. I don't want my first visit to their church to be one where Travis and his family will feel uncomfortable." Katie sighed a sigh of relief.

"Of course, they would never complain to me about it, but hopefully looking like everyone else, we can all enjoy the service—without being questioned, or people whispering and pointing at me."

"Will you and Travis be joining us for lunch afterwards?"

"Not today. Travis' church is having a fellowship luncheon after the service and he asked me to stay for it. I told him I would."

"Then, you'll probably spend the afternoon and possibly the evening at his home, so it is likely that you won't be home until later tonight" Martha hugged her *dochder*, hoping Katie wouldn't notice the tears trying to escape. "I hope you have a *gut* time."

"*Danki, Mamm.* Now I need to hurry to get dressed so I don't keep Travis waiting on me."

Travis arrived before Katie was dressed and ready to go. Fortunately, her *dat* was sitting on the porch and waved for Travis to join him.

"*Gudemariye,* Travis. Katie isn't ready to go yet. Would you like some breakfast, or a cup of *kaffe*?"

"Thank you. I had breakfast before I left home. My mom asked me to let you know that she'd like to have everyone come over for supper again soon."

"That sounds *gut*. I'll let Martha know. Just let Katie know what night is best for your family—and we'll be there."

Just then Katie stepped outside the house. "Sorry you had to wait on me. I'm ready now."

She leaned down to give her *dat* a hug. "I'll see you later, *dat*. *Mamm* says to let you know she has fresh *kaffe* and some cake for you."

Before he could speak, she quickly followed Travis down the steps and then he was helping her into the car.

Once Travis had pulled out and was heading to his church, he glanced over at Katie.

"You seemed to be in a hurry to leave..."

"*Jah*, I talked to *Mamm* and she said *Englischer* clothes would be *gut* to wear today, but I wasn't sure how *Dat* would feel, and I didn't think we had time to discuss it or I would make you late to church."

"Is it okay if I tell you how pretty you look today. You always look nice no matter what you're wearing."

Travis pulled into the church parking lot. Leaning over, he kissed Katie's cheek. "Thank you for coming to church with me. I feel blessed because I get to spend the day with you—not just a few hours, but the entire day."

Katie smiled as she waited for him to walk around to open her door. She was looking forward to today, too.

Katie was surprised to see so many people she knew who attended the baptist church that Travis and his family were members.

Mr. and Mrs. O'Neal were there, Ada Mueller, Ethan Lewis, John Baker, and the mayor and his wife were among those she noticed. The biggest surprise was finding Richard Anderson attending—and participating in the choir.

The music was lovely. The pastor brought a simple, but heart-warming message to the people. At the end, while someone was quietly playing the piano, the pastor offered to pray for anyone needing prayer. When the service ended, he gave a short prayer thanking God for his blessings, then he dismissed everyone. But before anyone could leave, he reminded everyone of the fellowship luncheon and welcomed visitors to stay and join them.

It seemed like most everyone there found time to come up to meet Katie. Bobby stayed close by for a while, then ran off to play with some of the boys his age. Gwen stuck close to Katie, only leaving her a few times to help in the church kitchen.

Sean was there, too. Katie was a bit surprised, after he ran the Irish Blessings Cafe all week, when he volunteered to help in the kitchen today. He was truly a blessing to his Uncle Andrew.

After a simple supper meal that Gwen and her mom prepared, Katie stayed a while to work a puzzle with Bobby and Trevor. Travis stayed close by, chatting with Sean about what was happening at work the next week.

He watched Katie, and when she looked like she was getting tired, he quickly said goodbye, put his phone away, and asked Katie if she was ready to leave.

When she nodded her head, he waited while she said goodbye to his mom and siblings, then he led her toward his car.

"I don't want to take you home exhausted, Katie-girl. If you ever want to leave sooner, just let me know."

"I'm fine. You know how I hate leaving your house."

"I know, but Mondays are usually busy, and I want you to get plenty of rest tonight. I'll miss our walk around the lake, but I think I should let you go early so you'll be ready for tomorrow."

Arriving at the Chupp farm, he signaled, then turned into the driveway. Once he parked, he noticed that her parents were not sitting on the porch, as they often did.

Leaning over, he kissed her. "Did I tell you how lovely you look in your *Englischer* clothes? I can't decide if I prefer the pretty dress or the jeans..."

Kissing her again, he sighed. "If you want me to be honest, I guess the dress is the best choice for church, because the jeans tend to umm, get me... umm. Well my thoughts sometimes get a bit out of control when I see you in a tight pair of jeans."

Instead of getting offended, Katie giggled. She reached up to touch his lips, then moved her hand to his neck and pulled his face down to hers and kissed him, then moved to whisper in his ear. "I'm glad. Because your tight jeans sometimes give me improper thoughts, too."

Turning and opening her door, she looked back at him with a big smile, then ran for the house. By the time Travis was out of his seat belt and opening his door, she turned to wave to him, then went inside and closed the door.

Travis closed his car door, and with a goofy grin

on his face, drove home.

twelve

The next week went by quickly. Then another. And another. Before Hannah knew it, it was November and the weather was definitely getting colder now. She and Richard were getting along well. He usually came in early. Sometimes he even beat her to the shop and was waiting patiently for her to arrive.

He had been helping her since Mr. Dell had left. There wasn't anything he wouldn't do, including taking out the trash, washing dishes or mopping the floor. When she tried to tell him he didn't need to come in so early or stay late to help clean up, he laughed.

"Now Hannah, when I said I wanted to learn everything, I meant it. I've even snuck over to the Irish Blessings Cafe a few times to talk to Andrew and Sean about how they handle their jobs at the cafe."

"I just don't want you to think I can't handle doing everything, because I truly can. I promise I won't let you down. If you want me to do anything differently, just let me know and I'll make the changes you want done, without any problems."

"Nope, there aren't any changes right now. That's not to say in the future, we may want to tweak things a bit, but only if you and I agree that it's a good thing for the shop—and the customers."

Charles Dell, the previous owner, had written to Richard several times, and he always brought the letters to work to share with Hannah.

"Look, Hannah. Charles took his brother Ben to the Magic Kingdom a few weeks ago. He says they had a great time there. They rode the rides, bought a few souvenirs, stayed to see the fireworks at the end."

"He even bought two stuffed toys... one for Bella's daughter, and one for Freida's son. They both agreed it was a wonderful experience—but once is probably enough for them."

"And when Charles discovered that Ben was a big fan of the Potter book series, they went to the neighboring park, where there's an entire area dedicated to the school or the castle... I'm not sure which. And the nearby village. He said the village has shops, where Charles bought his brother a stuffed owl and a puff-something. Then they rode the train, which is on track nine and three quarters. Charles said they both had such a good time, they couldn't choose which park was more fun."

"Ben also bought a complete set of the movies, plus several souvenirs. They seemed to enjoy watching the other visitors as much as they did the actual park. They said people came dressed in costumes, with wands, and everyone was having a good time."

A customer came in, then another, then several more. After they left, Richard continued chatting about Charles and his brother. He seemed amazed that two retired gentlemen would have such a good time doing things they had never done before, but were doing now since Charles had moved in with his brother.

"Hannah, do you think you'd enjoy going

someplace like that? Do you—are you allowed—to read fiction books with magical aspects, such as wands, spells, things of that sort?"

"*Jah*, we are allowed to read the books and even see the movies, but generally only during our *rumschpringe*. It's not encouraged, but it is allowed."

"Are you still having your *rumschpringe* or is it over? How long does something like that last? How exactly does it work?"

As another customer walked in, Hannah quickly took their order and chatted with them for a couple of minutes. After they had left, she looked over at Richard. "If you still want to know about *rumschpringe*, we can talk about it now."

"Yes, I do."

"Well, *rumschpringe* generally starts around age seventeen, and it ends when the person chooses to be baptized and joins the church—or they might choose to leave the church. Someone can be on *rumschpringe* for years."

"For some reason, I thought it would be more structured, with specific times to start and end... and lots of rules."

"It's our time to make certain that we want to join the church. Once we join, we can never leave—or we'll be shunned by everyone in the church. So we need to take as much time as we need until we know for sure what is best for us."

She sighed. "A lot of teens leave the church, but that's the whole point of it. And there aren't really any rules, although most parents try to keep their teens from going too crazy. Some have gotten in trouble with the law—and that's never *gut*."

"Are you still having your *rumschpringe* or is it over? Did you chose to join the church?" He looked closely at her. "Am I being too nosy? You don't have to tell me if you don't want to."

Hannah felt like she was blushing. She hoped not. "*Nee*, I don't mind telling you." She paused a moment before continuing. "I am still on my *rumschpringe*. Perhaps I should have already joined the church... I always expected to... but something is holding me back."

Hannah wiped down the counter where she was standing, waiting for another customer to come in. She looked over at Richard, who was watching her. She wasn't sure why, but she enjoyed talking to him about it.

He almost looked like it was something important —that it might affect her job. Would he let her continue working if she left the church—or joined the church?

"I've talked to Katie and Freida about it, since they're my best friends. Freida joined the church before she married Thomas, and Katie seems to be waiting for a sign, like me. They both gave me the advice to not rush, but to make certain what I felt was the best decision."

"See, as long as I don't join the church, I can still be accepted in the community and in people's homes, but if I were to join, then leave, I would probably leave town because I would always be shunned."

She walked a little closer to him. "I guess I should ask you if my decision could or would affect my job here. I don't want to lose my job. But deciding to join the church or not is a choice that I feel *Gott* is leading me to do."

Richard carefully patted her arm. "I'm a little concerned that you'll be asked to quit if you join the church, but please don't think I would ask you to stay or leave, or influence your decision. As long as the church allows you to work here, you are welcome to stay as long as you want."

As the little bell over the door rang, in walked a couple of customers. Hannah hurried back to the counter to help them.

After The Coffee Cup closed, Richard washed up the dishes, then got the trash ready to take outside to the dumpster behind the shops. Just before he walked outside, he asked Hannah if she would stay a few minutes after the cleanup was done so he could talk to her about something.

Hannah wondered what her boss wanted with her. She thought back to what they discussed earlier, but he had said everything was fine. She quickly finished up and sat down at the table close to the window, where they usually sat whenever they had things to discuss.

Almost immediately Richard came out of the back, where he had been opening boxes of supplies they would need the next morning.

"First, I want to assure you that you have a job here, no matter what, for as long as you want one."

Hannah almost wanted to cry. She really liked her new boss, but he seemed a bit upset. Why were they having this meeting if he wants her to stay?

"Whoa! Hannah! I didn't mean to upset you."

"I'm not upset."

"I can tell you are. Let me please have my say, and I promise I won't ever mention it again. It's just that I talked to Andrew and Amelia about this, and they thought I should just ask you."

"Ask me what?"

Now Richard looked a bit sheepish. "It's just... well, is there any chance—any chance at all—that you would consider... um... going on a date? With me?

thirteen

Richard felt terrible! First he had embarrassed Hannah, then he had upset her. He finally blurted out what he had wanted to ask her—and probably scared her off. She'd never consider dating him now, even if he begged her to.

"Oh my dear, I am so very sorry. I feel like a clumsy clod. If there was the slightest chance that you were ever going to give me a chance, I've ruined it. I wouldn't blame you if you never wanted to see me again."

Hannah looked slightly shocked. "You're asking me to go on a date with you?"

"Well... yeah." Richard cleared his throat. "That is, there's a theater not too far from here that is playing those Potter movies. I think I asked you before if you were a fan, but I don't remember your answer."

"Anyway, I thought you might be interested in going... and I'd be honored to take you. A movie theater is a place you should go to with a friend—not alone. Of course, you may want to go with one of your friends. You might not have any desire to go anywhere with me."

Hannah opened her mouth, but Richard quickly jumped in, not really giving her a chance to speak.

"I shouldn't have asked. I'm your boss—and several years older than you. Of course you wouldn't be interested in going to a movie... or out to dinner... with me."

"Richard," Hannah held her hand up, almost touching his nose. "Give me a chance to speak, please."

"Of course... Of course." He sat quietly, waiting for her to go on.

"Just answer my question. Did you ask me... to

go with you... on a date?"

"Uh... yeah. I mean yes."

"Are you asking strictly as a friend? Or as a potential suitor?"

"Oh, whichever one you prefer is fine with me."

"But that doesn't answer my question. If I'm going to date an *Englischer*, I need to know if *you* want to go to dinner or a movie as friends... or if *you* want to date me." Hannah let that sink in a minute, then went on. "Let me see if I can help... I am not interested in going out to dinner or a movie with you. As friends."

When Richard looked confused, Hannah continued. "If I'm going to go out with an *Englischer*, it will only be because he has feelings for me and wants to date me. If you don't know for sure, we should wait until you are certain why you're asking me on a date."

She stood up and walked out the door—without looking back.

She knew Ada Mueller lived a couple of blocks away, so she hurried along, hoping to get to her house and call John Baker, who could drive her home.

Richard felt like an idiot. Realizing Hannah rushed out the door, into a dark street, he quickly turned out the lights, locked the door, and hurried after her.

Oh no, which way did she go?

He knew she hadn't passed the window, so he took off in the opposite direction, hoping to catch up to her. He was passing the first side street when he saw a figure walking in that direction.

Quickly he ran after her. Hoping not to frighten her, he called out softly to her.

"Hannah, is that you? Please wait for me. I need to talk to you."

Hannah knew she couldn't outrun Richard. Rather than allow him to continue running after her, she stopped and waited for him to catch up.

"Hannah, where are you going?"

"I was going to Ada's house to use her phone to call John Baker to drive me home."

"I can do that. You don't need to call someone else to drive you home. Let me do that."

"*Danki.* I will let you take me home."

Richard escorted Hannah back to the shop. He usually parked his SUV behind the shop. Once they had walked around the building to it, he held the door while she got in and fastened her seat belt.

It was mostly quiet on the drive home. When Richard pulled into their driveway, he shut off the engine and turned to face Hannah.

"Hannah, you are the first person I've found myself really attracted to in a long time. I've wanted to ask you out for a while, but wanted to give you time to get to know me. I'm sorry I made a mess of tonight."

"I guess I should have been more patient. I'm not usually like that. Really."

"Let me answer your questions please. Yes, I am very attracted to you. Yes, I want to date you with the intent of getting to know you better and hopefully becoming a couple in the near future. And no, we don't have to see a movie. I would love to take you someplace for dinner."

"Well, I would love to accept your invitation to dinner if you would like to invite me to dinner..."

"Hannah, would you please allow me to take you to dinner tomorrow night after The Coffee Cup closes?"

"*Jah*, I would enjoy that very much..."

fourteen

Sunday, December the first, was a beautiful day...
it had begun snowing just before dawn, and a light
snow continued to fall during the day.

Many of Hannah's friends would be attending the
morning worship service with her at the Abbott Creek
Baptist Church, then a light meal would be served in
the church's fellowship hall.

Afterwards, Hannah and her best friend Katie
would freshen up, change clothes and prepare to join
the others, including Richard and Charles Dell, who

had come up on the train with his brother Ben.

Hannah had lost her parents in a buggy accident, when a truck had hit a patch of ice. Hannah had been only sixteen and the community had surrounded her with love and support.

Charles Dell had suddenly announced that he could no longer handle running The Coffee Cup by himself and had asked Hannah if she would like to come help him.

Ada Mueller had offered Hannah a place to live. Katie and several others in the community visited Hannah more often, making sure she had things she needed, and always had a ride to church events.

Hannah was a sweet person, and people were happy to invite her to their homes. She always seemed to make everyone around more joyful... peaceful... loved.

Today, everyone who was planning to stay for the special event—which looked to be everyone who had attended the morning worship service, in addition to many others in the community, were already in their seats, waiting patiently for the music to begin.

"Katie, am I supposed to be *naerfich*? Because I'm not—I'm really not. I never imagined this would happen to me... and so quickly. But it did, and we just couldn't find a good reason to wait any longer."

"I think if you feel ready, then it's the perfect time. I wish I felt the same way as you. Sometimes I feel if I don't hurry up and decide whether or not to join the church, I'm going to lose Travis."

"Oh, Hannah. I don't know what I'd do if I lost Travis, I truly don't." Katie sniffed, then pulled out a tissue and wiped her eyes. "Oh no! Why did I bring this up now? I don't want to ruin your day."

"Katie, you couldn't ruin my day, no matter what. Let's talk about this a few more minutes." Hannah had a thoughtful look in her eyes. "Now, leaving your feelings—and Travis' feelings—out of it, how much do you worry about disappointing your family... and your community?"

"Actually, quite a lot. No matter which decision I make about the church, I will be disappointing too many people. I can't do it! I can't make a decision at all!"

Hannah laughed. "Of course you would feel that way. I know just what you mean. But... now, for just a moment, close your eyes, don't think about anyone else. Concentrate only on your feelings. Which decision is the right one? Which decision is the one that will make you happy?"

The knock at the door startled them, causing them to giggle. Katie rushed to give her friend a hug.

"*Danki,* Hannah. I know what to do now. It's the only thing I can do. I don't know why I thought I was confused before." The girls hugged again.

"By the way, can I be the first to tell you how *wunderbaar* you look... oh, and thank you for picking out such a nice *Englischer* dress for me to wear."

Hannah hugged her friend again.

"Now," Katie smiled. "We're holding everything up, so we've got to get out there. Are you ready?"

"I'm ready... and now I'm getting a little *naerfich,* so let's do this before everyone out there decides to leave before we get there."

"The first person Katie saw when she entered the church was Travis, standing beside Richard, who was looking on top of the world. The two men were wearing new suits and looked very nice. When the music playing changed to the wedding march, Katie reached the front and turned around in time to see Hannah walking down the aisle.

Ach, she looked beautiful. In Katie's Amish community, couples usually married on Tuesdays or Thursdays, which were the least busy days. But most *Englischers* seemed to prefer the weekend.

When she reached the front, Hannah turned and passed her bouquet to Katie to hold until the service was finished.

Hannah and Richard were keeping everything simple, so everyone, including their Amish friends, would meet at the Schmidt farm to congratulate the happy couple.

Cake and ice cream would be served, then the couple had asked Travis and Gwen Davis to watch over The Coffee Cup while they took a week's long honeymoon

Once they were back, Hannah would move into Richard's home. Then they would return to The Coffee Cup, where they would continue to work together.

As the music stopped and the ceremony began,

Katie smiled at Travis, who was watching her, then she turned her attention to Richard and Hannah...

fifteen

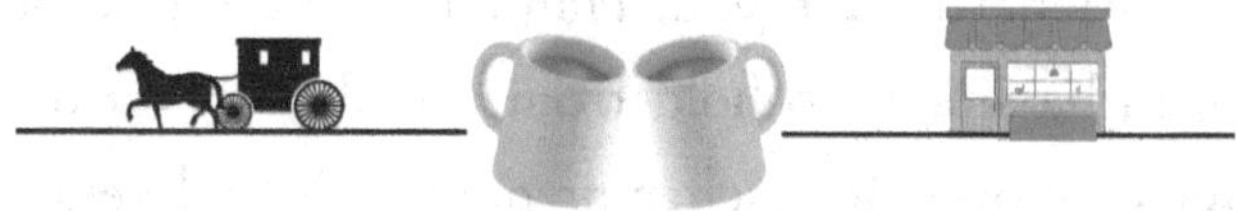

Dearly beloved, we are gathered here today, in the presence of God, to join Hannah Marie Kaufmann and Richard David Anderson in Holy Matrimony.

Richard, do you take this woman to be your wedded wife, to live together in holy matrimony? Do you promise to love her, honor her, comfort and keep her, forsaking all others, for as long as you both shall live?

"I do."

Hannah, do you take this man to be your wedded husband, to live together in holy matrimony,? Do you promise to love him, honor him, comfort and keep him, forsaking all others, for as long as you both shall live?

"I do."

"Richard, you may repeat your vows…"

"I Richard, take you, Hannah, to be my wedded wife, to have and to hold from this day forward, for better or worse, for richer or poorer, in sickness and in health, to love, honor, and cherish, 'til death do us part."

"Hannah, you may repeat your vows…"

"I Hannah, take you, Richard, to be my wedded husband, to have and to hold from this day forward, for better or worse, for richer or poorer, in sickness and in health, to love, honor, and cherish, 'til death do us part."

After the giving and receiving of rings, and lighting the unity candle, Richard and Hannah turned back to face their pastor.

"Richard and Hannah, insomuch as you have consented together in holy wedlock, and have witnessed the same before God and these witnesses, I now pronounce you husband and wife. Richard, you may kiss your bride."

Richard looked at his beautiful bride, noting a few tears on her cheeks. He leaned forward and kissed her—a perfect kiss.

"And now, it is my honor to introduce to you, Mr. and Mrs. Anderson."

TURN THE PAGE
FOR EXCLUSIVE
BONUS CONTENT

KEEP READING FOR A SNEAK PEEK OF BOOK TWO IN THE SERIES:

WARM PEPPERMINT WISHES

one

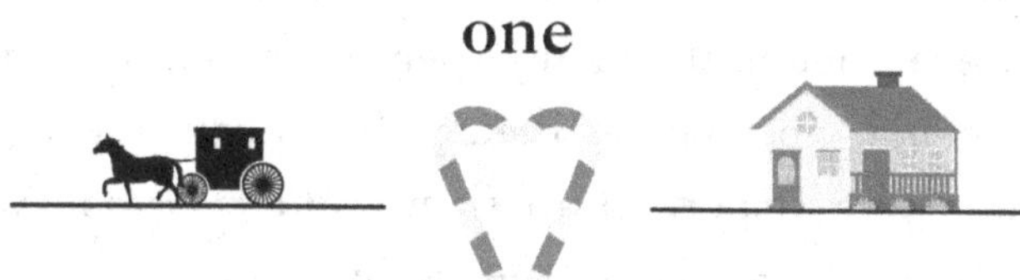

Monday morning found Jacob Yoder and his *bruders* Thomas, and Timothy busily working on the two houses that were currently being built on the Yoder farm.

Thomas' house had been started during the previous spring, and the foundation had been finished by the end of summer. However, while working on the foundation, his twin *bruder* Timothy had decided he wanted to start building his own house, and he'd let it be known that it needed to be done by the end of the year—or sooner—if possible.

So now here it was... the second week of December, and they were working on two houses instead of one. No one knew for sure if the houses would be done and ready to move into on time, but most everyone in the family spent every spare minute they could working on them. They knew the boys' homes were important to them, and everyone was going to try to get them done on time.

Thomas' *frau,* Freida, was especially anxious to get moved into their house. Since their marriage two years ago, they had been living in the *daudi* house on the Yoder farm. It was nice and cozy, but quite small.

Last September their first child had been born... a *buwe* named Tobias, named after their bishop. Tobias was a sweet, captivating child, and a blessing to Freida and Thomas.

Freida never complained about living in the *daudi* house, but Thomas knew it was difficult for her to find room for the three of them—especially since Tobias had begun walking.

Unknown to all but a couple of friends, they had discovered a couple of months ago that they were expecting their second child, who was due the following May.

The *daudi* house was much too small for four people, so Thomas was determined to get his family moved into their new home before the new *bopli* arrived. If his family knew about the *bopli*, they would put his house above his brother's and get it done pronto.

But his *frau* didn't want to tell the others until Christmas. She figured it would be a *wunderbaar* surprise for everyone. Thomas was happy to go along with her plan, but it did make things a bit more difficult for him, especially when his *dat* kept asking what the hurry was to get moved.

Thomas also knew that in a few months, they would be busy working outside in the fields, and making repairs on the buildings and fences once winter was over. They wouldn't have time to work on the houses, so it needed to be finished before the end of winter, if at all possible.

"Hey *bruder*, with the foundation, framing, subfloors, and roof trusses done, plus the kitchen and bathrooms plumbed on my house, we're almost caught up to yours. We should have both roofs finished this week." Timothy looked excited about the news.

Thomas smiled back, stopping to look around at the houses they had been working on for months.

"And the rest of the work can be done inside once the roof is done, so even if there's bad weather it shouldn't slow us down much." Jake said, stopping for a moment to rest.

"Is this when Freida needs to decide what color paint she wants and picks out the appliances, furniture, and such that she needs?" Thomas asked his *bruders*.

Jake laughed. "Last time I talked to Mamm, she said Freida had already made all her decisions. She's just waiting for us to get done."

"I had no idea." Thomas said. "So who picked out the colors and appliances and everything for your house when we built it?"

"*Vell,* since I don't have a *frau*, I asked *Mamm* to make suggestions. I made a few changes, but not much. She was a *wunderbaar* help to me."

Jake continued, "As a matter of fact, Freida did the *schmart* thing... she asked her *mamm* to come by, then they got with our *mamm* and talked it all out and made a list of what Freida liked best. *Mamm* was *froh* that your *frau* was so thoughtful to include them both."

The three *buwes* laughed at how Freida had included both Sarah Schmidt and Ida Yoder, making them both feel special.

"That's my *frau*." Thomas bragged. "She's the

sweetest, most thoughtful *frau* in the world. And also the best *mamm*. Tobias gets to see her *mamm* and our *mamm* as much as he wants—or maybe I should say as much as they want. Either way... Tobias and his *mammis* seem *froh* with all the visits."

"*Gott* blessed you with such a *wunderbaar frau*. And now it's up to us to get her a house she can move around in. She's been more than patient, but I get the feeling that she's gonna be needing more space sooner rather than later."

"I have no idea what you could be talking about—and if I did, I am sworn to secrecy, so you just keep your ideas and opinions to yourself, and don't be getting me into trouble with my *frau*."

Timothy looked a little perplexed. "What are you both talking about?"

"Don't you be minding what your nosy *bruder* is talking about. I'm telling you both to keep anything you know—or think you know—to yourselves."

Anyone looking at the big grin and delighted look in his eyes would know something wunderbaar was expected, but his bruders knew how to keep secrets.

"Allrecht *buwes*, let's get up on this roof and get done before the sun gets hot in the sky. We've got a job to do."

Laughing and joking, the three *buwes* went back to work.

Meanwhile, Freida Yoder had delivered a sleepy Tobias to his *mammi* Ida and was headed to The Sweet Shop, where she would work the morning with her best friend, Katie Chupp.

It was a beautiful Monday morning, and Freida enjoyed Knowing her *mann* was at their new house, working to get it ready for his family to move into. Thomas was such a blessing! She knew he was doing everything he could to get their house done on time.

And it didn't help, that if the community were told about the new addition to their family, much of the men in the community would come out to help, making certain it was done quickly. With their help, it wouldn't take long at all. But Freida so wanted to surprise everyone at Christmas—and Thomas was determined to give her what she wanted.

So Thomas kept their secret. Nothing was said to anyone, and Thomas, along with his *dat* and his bruders, continued to work on his house—and his *bruder's* house—whenever they could spare the time.

Freida liked that she was doing her part to help her *mann*. Both her *mamm* and Thomas' *mamm* asked to have Tobias to visit often, so she would let him visit them three or four mornings each week, while she worked with Katie at the bakery. This was *gut* for several reasons...

First, she was making money each week to add to their savings, which would help purchase the appliances and furniture for their house. Thomas insisted she keep some of it for herself, but she usually spent most of it on him or Tobias.

Second, it helped at the bakery. She had worked there full-time until she married Thomas, so she had been trained and knew the routine. Some days she helped in the kitchen area, baking cookies and cakes alongside Katie. Other days she took customer's orders and rang them up.

Another benefit was getting to visit with those coming to the bakery to purchase items. It also gave her a chance to get out of the house for a few hours during the day, plus Tobias got to spend time at the Yoder house and the Schmidt house.

Her *mamm* had confided to her that when Tobias

visited, his *dawdi* usually found time to come back to the house for *kaffe* and to play with the wee *buwe*. Her *dat* was a *wunderbaar dawdi* and with her *bruders*, Marvin and David helping out at the farm whenever they could, her *dat* could take it a little easier—at least during the winter months.

Come spring, he became like a young *buwe* again, working out in the fields and helping his *frau* plant a large garden. Her *mamm* assured Freida they would have plenty of crops, the Lord willing, to share with all three of their *kinner* and their families. Freida was looking forward to helping her whenever she could. And she loved fresh, ripe just-picked vegetables.

Arriving at the bakery, Freida waved at Travis Davis, who was leaving to make deliveries. As she stepped inside, she took a moment to pray...

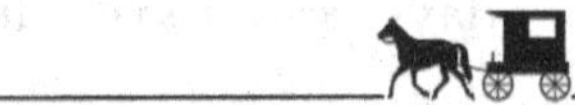

Thank you, *Gott*, for such a *wunderbaar* day. Help us to be a blessing to all who come to the bakery today. Bless Hannah and Richard as they begin a new life together. Bless Katie and Travis as they make one of the most important decisions of their lives. Protect our families—especially those working on the houses today. And bless our church leaders, especially our young bishop and his family. And please bless and protect our wee, new *kind*.

In Jesus' name,

Amen.

____

Acknowledgments

To God be the glory! HE is THE AUTHOR of my life! God gives me the inspiration for each and every book... books of family, faith, forgiveness, and grace...

When God placed it on my heart to write a light-hearted mystery series, I'm glad I obeyed... And when HE kept after me to write about a serious occurrence happening not only on school campuses, but in unexpected places, too, I struggled with it, but with lots of prayers and tears, it's finally done.

Thanks to Rachel, who not only designs my covers, memes, posters (well, you get the picture), but is also an amazing author and inspirational speaker.

Rachel, I couldn't have done it without you!

Thanks to Gwendolyn, who takes care of me when I need help, encourages me when I'm down, and keeps me moving.

Gwennie, God has truly blessed me with an incredible granddaughter!

Last, but by no means least, thank you to my awesome readers, who do so much to encourage me, support my writing, and continue to make my books a success!

ABOUT THE AUTHOR

Naomi Miller mixes up a batch of intrigue, sprinkled with Amish, Mennonite, and English characters, adding a pinch of mystery, and a dash of romance!

Naomi's days are spent focusing on her writing, editing and spending time with her family. She enjoys her career as an author, blogger and inspirational speaker.

She schedules several book events each year and enjoys the opportunity to meet readers face-to-face. When she's not rushing to meet a deadline, Naomi loves to make time to attend writing conferences, workshops, and other author events.

She is a former member of the American Christian Fiction Writers organization (ACFW) and the Authors Guild of Tennessee (AGT).

Whenever time permits, Naomi can be found in one of two favorite places. . . the beach and the mountains.

Naomi loves traveling with her family, singing inspirational/gospel music, taking daily walks, and witnessing to others of the amazing grace of Jesus Christ.

AUTHOR LINKS

WEBSITE: https://naomimillerauthor.com
FACEBOOK:
www.facebook.com/NaomiMillerAuthor
INSTAGRAM:
https://twitter.com/AuthorNaomi
PINTEREST:
http://www.pinterest.com/authornaomi
GOODREADS: http://bit.ly/1VMIegX
INDIEBOUND: http://bit.ly/1PsB9MR
FICTION FINDER: http://bit.ly/1UOlI5P

Katie Chupp arrives for work on what seems like a normal morning - only to discover that a disaster has taken over the bakery . . .

Not only do she and her co-workers have quite the mess to deal with - they must figure out who destroyed all of their hard work and trashed the bakery.

What will they do about the mess? How will they find out who is responsible? Will they be able to replace their lost orders . . . save the holiday festivities . . . and keep the intruder from continuing their breaking and eating spree?

It's Christmas time in Abbott Creek, and who would expect a mystery... or even two... to pop up and interrupt Katie while she tries to keep up with the Holiday rush?

With a winter chill settling in and Christmas right around the corner, no one would expect a mystery, but a mystery does indeed appear...

Katie Chupp is spending her days catering to the holiday rush, but she soon finds herself in the midst of a secret project that attracts more attention than she wants.

And when one local family finds a very unexpected surprise at their door, this is one mystery that may never be solved... even by Katie.

Amelia Simpkins may be a great cook, and have a head for business, but sweet treats are out of her league and the owner of the Irish Blessings Cafe says it's because she adds the tart to the Sweet Shop's new dessert that Katie Chupp insists is only filled with lemony goodness.

The two shop owners' constant bickering sends sparks flying through Abbott Creek's usual calm... and when Andrew's cafe suffers from some rather unusual pest problems, the town starts taking sides.

This is one mystery Katie wants no part of. But working for Mrs. Simpkins may put her in the middle – whether she intends to take sides . . . or not.

In the small town of Abbott Creek, mystery is as much a part of daily life as The Sweet Shop's Pumpkin pies.

Katie Chupp spends her days at The Sweet Shop. . . baking for the upcoming holidays and enjoying the changing seasons.

Thanksgiving is approaching and the residents of Abbott Creek are preparing to give thanks for their blessings.

But between fielding questions from every person in town who is desperate to find out where Mrs. Simpkins has gone, to finding extra help for the busy holiday season, Katie's blessings this year are being outweighed by her problems.

When a stranger comes to town looking for work, will it be an answer to Katie's prayers or spell trouble at The Sweet Shop?

Katie Chupp is not the only person in Abbott Creek looking forward to the most romantic holiday of the year.

But Valentine's Day will not be all hearts and flowers. There are secrets to be kept, feelings to be explored, and difficult decisions to be made — and each one has something to do with the heart.

Will those secrets come between friends? Will the happy couples in Abbott Creek get to celebrate. . . together? With the demand for sweet treats fierce this year. will the Sweet Shop's baker find time for romance?

And will one young woman be able to live with the choice she must make on the most romantic day of the year?

Things are changing in Abbott Creek. . .

Between babies and budding romances, busy schedules and unexpected gossip, the small town and its residents may never be the same.

Everyone at the Sweet Shop Bakery and the Irish Blessings cafe is worrying over Bella and her baby – and busily trying to convince her to take it easy.

Katie is not the only person in town with some big decisions ahead of her. And the busy summer season is kicked off with a big surprise for everyone.

Don't miss the revelation everyone has been waiting for – in Peach Cobbler Mystery.

Naomi Miller

Katie and her friends in Abbott Creek enjoy cooking . . . and baking, and they would like to share some of their favorite recipes with you. They have gathered the best and most delicious recipes to be found in Abbott Creek, and added in some fun extras to go along with them. That way, you can enjoy reading about your favorite characters while you enjoy their favorite treats.

Could love soften Leah's heart so that she is able to see her answered prayers in Naomi Yoder or will she drive a wedge between her father and the only woman he has shown interest in since Elisabeth Fisher's death?

Leah Fisher lost her mother ten years ago. She is rapidly approaching womanhood and the lack is becoming more difficult every day.

Will she be able to recognize love when it's right in front of her?

Could love be the key to Leah opening her heart, making room for the woman her father intends to marry... or will she stubbornly cling to the memory of her own mother?

It's Christmas time in Abbott Creek, and who would expect a mystery... or even two... to pop up and interrupt Katie while she tries to keep up with the Holiday rush?

With a winter chill settling in and Christmas right around the corner, no one would expect a mystery, but a mystery does indeed appear...

Katie Chupp is spending her days catering to the holiday rush, but she soon finds herself in the midst of a secret project that attracts more attention than she wants.

And when one local family finds a very unexpected surprise at their door, this is one mystery that may never be solved... even by Katie.

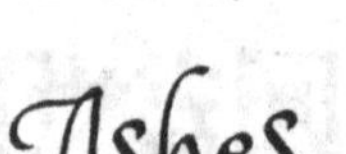

NAOMI   RUTH
MILLER   MILLER

What if . . . the Little Cinder Girl was Amish . . .

Fix dinner, Ella. Clean the House, Ella. Get the shoes fixed, Ella.

Ella is different than most young women in town. She would rather read than watch television. She values kindness over popularity, and she secretly wishes for a family who actually wants her around.

Ella has faced loss and tragedy, and yet she keeps a sweet, brave face, no matter how difficult life becomes.

This is a story about kindness, courage, and finding lost loved ones.

Ashes to Amish is a plain retelling of the much beloved Cendrillon by Charles Perrault... with an English twist.

This is the story of how a sweet, shy kitten found two children and decided they would be her new family. Read along with Sammy and Macy as they tell the story of finding a little lost kitten, naming her, loving her, and making her part of their (or rather, becoming her own) family.

This is the story of Sophie's first Thanksgiving with her new family. Read along with Sammy and Macy as they tell the story of changing seasons, going back to school, preparing for cooler weather, and celebrating the day of giving thanks with the newest member of their family.

This is the story of how a sweet, shy kitten found two children and decided they would be her new family.Read along with Sammy and Macy as they tell the story of finding a little lost kitten, naming her, loving her, and making her part of their (or rather, becoming her own) family.